I0557041

MY TORMENTED MAGE

MIKI WARD

GARRETT WARD

My Tormented Mage
A Ceorfan Gargoyles Novella

Cover Design by Nikki Morris Thompson at KT Graphic Design /Editing by Erica
Collins
Formatted by Vicki M Duran

CONTENTS

NOTE FROM THE AUTHORS

We dedicate this book to our families.
-Miki & Garrett

TO OUR READERS...

Thank you for purchasing this book and reading it! Please don't be afraid to leave a review if you like it. We hope you as the readers enjoy this book as much as we enjoyed writing it. Be warned: It is a dark fantasy and recommended for ages 18+. This book contains graphic sex scenes, violence, paranormal events, and language.

Sincerely Yours,
Miki Ward and Garrett Ward

MY TORMENTED MAGE

By

Miki Ward & Garrett V Ward

1

A WARM NIGHT

THE MOON IS FULL AND HIGH IN THE NIGHT SKY. EVEN UNDER the trees where they lie on the sand they can see it. It's early in the morning, still dark but the moon is bright. The September night warm near the city of Ageum. Kick and Drusey came to the secluded area of the waterfront to be alone. "It's marvelous here and I love it, what do you think, Drusey?" Kick asks.

"Yes, it's beautiful. Hey, will you rub my shoulders?" She appeals and pouts at her tall mage warrior. He's gorgeous and she can't help ogling him. His black curls are pushed back from his face giving her full view of his dark eyes. He gazes back at her marveling at her beauty. The allure of this place only emphasizes her looks.

Watching her he gets wrapped up in the view. He couldn't care less that she's miniature for a warrior gargoyle. She is only five feet three inches tall, a plus for him, he towers over her. Anyone, without a clue, might believe they could overpower his girl in a fight, having firsthand knowledge that's a mistake. He's seen her in a scrap. A rage flares in her when she fights, even during combat training. When she fights she battles to win.

Kick audibly gulps as Drusey turns her sexy gargoyle body

toward him flirting. His heart skips a beat. Her tan skin has never experienced the light of day but is the color it would be if she spent hours soaking in the sun. Sandy blonde pieces of hair escape its braid and blows around her face as she pulls it in front of her. After rolling onto her side and turning toward him, she exposes her bare breasts. Instinctively he stares right at them, mouth open, eyes wide, and a stupid grin. Trying to behave, his focus travels up to the deep blue of her eyes. They're so deep they're almost purple and searching his own eyes.

"Come on, handsome, put your book down and rub my shoulders. We came to the shore to rest. I'm sore after our lessons in the arena. Please, will you put the textbook down and rub my back?" Her voice slides into a lower octave knowing the reaction it has on him.

Kick can't put down his spell book fast enough. Studying wasn't going well anyway he can't concentrate with her so close. He's sure she knows what she does to him and that he can't think straight seeing her topless.

"Of course, I'll rub your shoulders," Kick replies. *It gives me a reason to touch you.* With pleasure, he massages her back and wing arms using pressure techniques he studied in med school on her stiff muscles.

"Oh, that feels good," she moans. "What are you studying, anyway?"

Kick says, "Spells and more spells, that's all. Well, that's not all, we're learning new spells but also how to use them in the arena outside the castle. Did you know that castle Ilioilion is three hundred years old?" The castle is located within the walls of Ageum. The city while nearly four thousand years old is modern. They channel water throughout the city for sanitation and drinking. Although, it isn't the first city built in the area, it has been destroyed and rebuilt many times in its history. The last time was over three hundred years ago when another Greek city-state attacked and destroyed Ageum over a dispute involving the mother of Queen Iphigenia, Helen.

"No, I knew it was old, though. The castle is huge. Have you ever been inside?" Drusey asks.

"I've been in the castle on many occasions. When I was doing my medical education, I treated Queen Leta. That's how I started working there."

"Is it fancy inside the palace?" she asks excitedly.

"Yes, it is, not much has changed since I was first there either, except Iphigenia was the ruler then. It was before... well you understand." Kick stops, drops his head shaking it from side to side. The sadness in his eyes is obvious. Memories surface of the time in gargoyle history when Queen Iphigenia sacrificed her life to return the Ceorfan gargoyles to life. There were consequences, like turning to stone in the daylight. The Guild calls this process torpifying or torping. It's both blessing and curse—and the reason that the Ceorfan day begins when the sun goes down.

"Yes, I remember..." Drusey whispers.

He returns to the discussion about school, deflecting. "Did anyone ever tell you that the large arena is where we'll fight our acceptance battles into the Ceorfan Warrior Mage Guard?" That's the name of their school and will also be their job titles. If... they pass the rigorous schooling. Then they need to pass the virtually impossible tests plus receive the required number of referral documents. The Guild requires the Guard to be trustworthy and more than excellent soldiers. Graduation is nearing for Kick and Drusey, along with their classmates, they've gone to school for years. However, when they finish, their hardest training begins, improving their skills is a lifelong process on the job.

"Ouch, sorry, don't stop. I'm okay... just tweaked a nerve," Drusey cries.

"I'm sorry, I'll go easier. Did Peter hurt you in practice?" he asks. *I might need to talk to him about hurting my girl.*

Kick wasn't Drusey's partner in the arena tonight... again. Although the two of them don't know, the training masters figured out that he's in love with her and takes it easy on her. No way would she have learned half of what she did this evening if she had sparred with Kick. This evening she was matched with a smaller man, not weak by any stretch, named Peter. A larger gargoyle was Kick's partner his name is Kokkino Petra, or Kino as he's called. They had talked and found they have a lot in common. They're the largest of the cadet trainees. Both of their fathers are statesman working with the queen. They make perfect sparing partners. In their cases the Ceorfan statesmen have proven that they breed large sons.

Kick gently moves his lady's hair over, his big hands, covering the top of her small back and wings. He slides his hand down moving to other areas of her body. He skims down her sides, grazing the sides of her breasts, then down toward the small of her back and pushes at the band of her short skirt.

Before he starts something, he pleads, "Do you want to swim? Afterward we can get supper before you torp."

"Sounds fun! Last one in the water is a hydra!" she shouts jumping up running toward the water. As they reach the sea, Kick takes her hand and drags her with him. The waves climb above them and they dive into the cool water. The fluorescent wave, lit by the full moon, speeds past them. They surface in a trough between ripples, both laughing and looking into each other as they plunge into the next swell. Because of her gargoyle nature she doesn't suffer the sting of the cold. But he's half human and half fae it's a shock to his system for a few minutes as his body adjusts. The sea is wonderful though, and it helps loosen their strained muscles, aching from practice earlier. They float for a while, fit as they are, they're not easily tired. He moves close to her and pulls her to him gathering her close for a kiss.

Soon, he is going to ask for her hand. His parents are happy about the match. The queen said she thinks he'll be a wonderful husband for Drusey. Kick has been friends with Queen Leta of the Ceorfan since she was a teenager and he was a young medical student. He helped her once when she was sick. He's a confidant to Her Majesty now. The laws of the Ceorfan Guild are clear on marriages; Kick must have the approval of his queen and the parents. He loves Drusey but he's a little anxious that she doesn't feel the same. Yet, when she has her strong body pressed against his, he thinks she just might. He decides right that second to brave it and move forward with his plan and ask her.

"Drusey, I have time off this evening. Will you go with me to the caves later? I'll bring us some breakfast, then we can go to class and on to training. What do you think?"

"That is a great idea. I would enjoy it. Now, let's get home so I can pose before sunrise. Come watch so you can get some of my energy," Drusey returns. When a gargoyle hardens it releases magic energy which radiates from their bodies during the torping process, the ones they love are welcome to absorb that energy. It's a family type sharing and is a widely practiced part of this culture. As excited as Kick is, this energy will also help him stay awake to lay the groundwork for his plans for tonight.

With hope in his fast beating heart, they race to her home where they greet her parents. His beautiful lady walks to her posing stage, a raised platform in the corner of the living area. She steps up, and her parents join her there. They all say together smiling, "Wings up, have a healing sleep."

A warm tingle covers Kick as he soaks up the magic that the family radiates when they torpify to stone in front of him. It gives him all the strength he needs for his plan. He says, "Goodbye, Drusey."

The Ceorfan gargoyles heal during torpification, no matter how badly they are hurt—it's a gift. The young man stares at her hardened stone body and hopes his lady sees him regarding her. He nods goodbye to her parents, recognizing they can see and hear him if they are still awake then twists around and leaves.

2

HE BRAVED IT

Kɪᴄᴋ's ʙᴇᴇɴ ʙᴜsʏ sɪɴᴄᴇ ʟᴇᴀᴠɪɴɢ ᴛʜᴇ ʜᴏᴍᴇ ᴏғ ʜɪs ɢɪʀʟ. Hᴇ's been setting up his surprise for her. Actually, he's been working his butt off. Good thing he absorbed the magic when Drusey and her parents torped. He wants every detail perfect. Now, that the sun has set he's ready to pick her up. He's so edgy, he's almost skipping. When he notices he stops dead in his tracks and tries to look sexier. Almost there... he combs his fingers through his hair and blows on his palm to check his breath. As he rounds the corner he spots her waiting expectantly for him by her open front door. Kick gives her a hug, when he reaches her, then a kiss while trying to hide his nervousness. He partially succeeds.

As the two friends part their embrace, he removes a portal stone from the side pocket of his best blue tunic. As he does, he pauses briefly, careful to let her see but not seeking to entirely display his hidden gift. As hoped, Drusey catches sight of the stone, but continues to stare questioningly at his hand... the one holding the portal stone. In what seems like forever, he watches as recognition dawns in her gorgeous eyes. "I guess we're traveling somewhere?" she says in response to his hint and cocks a cagey eyebrow in his direction. Kick grins and waves a quick greeting to her family who are sitting outside on the porch.

Kick sings a spell opening a portal in front of them. Merriment washes over him as the portal dilates. Drusey continues to search his face, hoping to get another clue of what his plans are. He only sees her smile. It isn't a confused or even an approving smile. Yet, that's implied by her body language. It's the kind shared between lovers who also have a deep abiding friendship. He knows she would follow him anywhere right now, just to be together. More importantly, it indicates her unswerving trust in him. The thought melts his heart, and he smiles back before singing another short refrain which opens a door within the portal. He draws her toward him guiding her through the doorway to the set-up he toiled on all day.

"Oh Kick, oh Kick," she stammers as she turns in a circle, taking in the beautiful scene he had laid out. The warm air and the smell of the sea nearby imprints upon her mind. Her hopeful Eros has lined one of the caves on the coast near Ageum with candles. Awh! Inside the cave is a pond of turquoise water fed by an underground spring. The candles light up the water, its clarity allowing the light to diffuse across the bottom of the pond only to bounce it back around the room, lighting the room with a frosty green color.

Drusey excitedly spies a mat, a blanket, and a basket full of fruit and bread. There are also goblets and a skin of wine awaiting preparation as well.

"I bet you worked all day on this set-up. Did you sleep at all, Kick?"

"No!" he says a little too excitedly. "But, I feel fine. Do you like it?"

"Yes, Kick. I like it very much."

Kick has a manic amount of energy. He quickly lights the few candles that have gone out. Then he rapidly straightens the blanket on the mat. He takes Drusey by the hand, leading her to the blanket and helps her to sit. Then he takes his seat with her on the cover. His energy takes over, so he fills her a plate. She laughs at how much he's put on her plate, but graciously accepts without comment. He really does know what she likes.

After they have filled their bellies, Kick leans back on a stalagmite. Drusey rests her head on his chest and relaxes, enjoying the moment. A hair-clip in her bun presses into his chest. He removes it and drops it onto the blanket beside them as he pulls her hair away from her face. Playing with her hair he lets his fingers slide down the side of her neck and onto her breast, she unexpectedly jumps up, landing on her knees. Kick's heart crashes. Her rejection startles him. Kick was afraid of rejection by her, but he didn't think it would happen this fast. The sadness in his eyes clear as he looks up into hers.

She doesn't notice his mood. Kick silently wonders how he could've misread... In an instant, she's straddling his lap and giggling as she leans into him for a kiss. Her long locks spread over him. Her kisses are soft and travel over his upper body before returning her mouth to his. They deepen the kiss and his hips rock up into her, he holds her down into his thrust while she pushes back and moans.

Kick turns her over with a deft flip and begins removing her clothes. Her tight fighting apparel is easily removed in seconds. Pausing he devours her body with his eyes, appreciating her beauty. She's small and curvy and her muscles well defined from years of training. Kick has seen her nude many times, but it's always like the first time.

Soaking in her beauty, Kick feels his cock grow. The engorgement of his desire overwhelms him, and he can't wait. He stands to remove his own clothes, not touching her is torturous. She rises to her knees by pulling on his legs. On her knees before him, she looks up into his face. Her impish smile says everything. Leaning in she nips his leg. Her hot kisses begin inside each of his thighs working her way to his cock until she rolls her tongue around the head of it. Suddenly she sucks the top few inches into her wet mouth. With him in her mouth, she pulls his ass toward her, allowing his dick to push all the way into her mouth and down her throat some. She swallows, taking as much of him into her mouth as she can.

"Oh god, Fighter, you're good!" he groans. She pulls her head back, smirking. Before she can do anything else, he pushes her to the ground. He kisses her hard. His hand finds her hot pussy and inserts a finger. He works his kisses down her neck to her breasts, then to her stomach and finally, he's licking her clit while his fingers continue their work. She's close. "No, don't stop!" she demands.

He is on his knees above her now, so she takes his erection and she rubs the tip on her body. When he's at his limit of control, she guides him into her tightness, rocking back and forth. Almost immediately her body tightens for her oncoming orgasm. He feels her stiffen and pumps faster and harder. "Fuck me, Kick, Oh I'm coming!" She lets him know how he makes her feel with loud moans of ecstasy. She orgasms and calls his name into the warm night air. The squeezing on his cock is enough to finish him. He explodes right after her. Kick keeps moving inside her until the sensitivity stops them both.

She rolls over panting and lays her head on his pounding chest. As young and fit as they are, they still must catch their breath. Taking a deep breath then letting it go Kick declares, "I love you, Fighter." He has called her that since the day they met. She had stolen a pastry he was enjoying right out from under his nose. He told her he would fight her for it and she took him up on his dare. Him letting her win is his story...

Drusey lies on his chest, happy in the afterglow of his actions and his words.

They can't wait any longer and must be on their way, so both rise to dress. She teases him for how much he's wearing. "It looks like you are going to one of your father's Senatorial meetings!"

"Well, at least I don't look like I've just had sex," he teases back. The teasing continues for as long as they are dressing. They eat a few leftovers and laugh over their jokes. They share the memory of her stealing his pastry and the time they got lost during the Agapi Trials when they were teenagers as they prepare to leave. Kick reassures her that he'll clean up the cave before class tomorrow.

Kick pauses, his hands in his pockets and his head down. "Kick, what is it?" Drusey queries.

"Will you please be my bride and share my life forever? I'll do the best I can for you and any children we might have," Kick rattles off. While he is speaking, he tugs loose a locket with his family name on out of his pocket. Kick's visage has changed from lustful and joyful to serious. The puppy dog eyes he is making at her is a clue to how dangerous he is, always getting his way with her!

One thing about the Ceorfan when they marry it really is until death do they part. They can document the number of couples who have separated on one hand, and that's over generations. Kick sits in silence waiting nervously. The quiet stretches out until he can hear his own heart beating all too loudly. He thinks that Drusey is telling him no by her silence and he starts to pack up the basket, his shoulders slumping with rejection.

He says, "It's okay. If you want to stay friends, we can." He sighs. "I should have thought better. I'm sorry. I hope I didn't ruin our friendship. Forgive me. Just forget I said anything, please."

"What? No, never. I'm just in shock, Kick. I've never imagined anyone would ever want to marry someone like me. I'm a warrior mage to the bone. Not ladylike at all. I love you. Of course, I want to marry you. Yes! The answer is, yes!"

She reaches for him and wraps her arms around his neck kissing him, laughing and crying at the same time.

"Oh, my beautiful fighter, I was afraid you were upset and didn't want me, a warrior mage for the same reasons. I'm so glad. Come on, we have to hurry to class, we'll tell our parents afterward. They're happy and will be glad to know you accepted. Here let me put this on you."

"Wait, you've already told them?" she asks quizzically.

"Of course, I did. I've also spoken with our queen."

At that, Drusey arches an eyebrow. "You were really prepared."

"Yes, I love you and wanted this to be perfect."

"Kick, I'll love you until my final breath. You made this perfect. Thank you."

His grin is intoxicating, and she adopts it. Carefully, he puts his necklace around her neck claiming that they are one. This necklace is intended for people to see when they portal to class with happy hearts.

Everyone notices. They are the buzz of the school and are congratulated by their friends as they walk the hallways to their classes. They can't stop smiling even if they want to that won't happen, anyway. They're made for each other and will make a wonderful life together. Now if they can concentrate enough to get through school so they can let their parents know.

AT THE END OF PROFESSOR ORPHEUS' class Kick stops at the door, Drusey is waiting for him, the same as every other day. This is where they meet before heading to warrior training at the end of their magical instruction classes every day.

Kick glimpses Drusey first and asks, "Drusey would you like to go to your parents first as soon as practice is over?"

"Yes! That would be great. After we speak with my parents, we can speak with yours."

"I would like that. Let's clean up first after training, then we'll go to your parents' house and eat with them. Afterward, we'll go to my parents. My mother is making us dessert!"

"Sounds fun!" Drusey laughs.

Happy about their plans they separate and enter the arena. There they'll have to find a way to concentrate on their sparring partners. If they can't, this may not be a good night for them in the arena.

3

THE FIRST BATTLE

The Pit, as in the exercise arena, is situated near the fences of Castle Ilioilium. You could rest on the southwestern edge of the castle wall and watch most of the fights. It's an earth floor in places, soft sand or gravel in others. The Pit has pergola overlaid with a mix of seaweed and grass. The grass is periodically soaked to create different training conditions for the students. This evening the turfs aren't wet. That's good news for Kick. He hates training in the simulated rain conditions or getting mud in his hair. 'It makes me look like a withered prune on top.' He once declared to his friend Steen. The young lovers enter the field with the other pupils and check for their instructors. "Well, there is Commander Mega, I'll see you in a while, handsome," Drusey says and heads off. "Fight hard, love," Kick returns. He follows her ass as she races away.

The Pit is set up in four different 'periochi,' or sparing areas. Trainees work through each based on the goals of the instructor and the goals of the Guard. The four periochi are Physical which includes boxing, wrestling, and an Asian fighting style called SooBak. Ranging Weapons to include the bow, throwing knives, and dory spear. Close in Weapons which include the hammer, a xiphos sword, and mace and Magical which varies by the gifts of each trainee. Each pupil is expected to pass three of the four periochi. They must also 'master' at least one. Since this school is for mages who are gifted in the arts of war, one of the physical tasks is better to master first. Mastery of periochi can take up to seven years depending on skill.

Gortanik is a remarkable student. He mastered two forms of Magical by his fourth year and the art of SooBak in his sixth year. His mastery of SooBak so complete, he earned his nickname, Kick, due to the crushing blows he lands with his feet when he fights.

Even as a half-human, half-fae, Kick keeps up with his gargoyle counterparts. Kick's size being larger than the average human makes him a challenging opponent to all but the goyles. Kick's gift and his first Magical mastery is his ability to Changer-Finder which is a rare combination. So far, he hasn't come upon a situation he's unable to change or anything he can't find. This gift lets Kick envision, a way to change minor things that are happening at the time, like his mother, who is an Empath with supernatural knowledge. She is able to help people with things of future importance. His mom is a priestess in the temple of Athena where she ministers to the masses. His changer gift only operates in an adaptation of the present. He can't change big things like the weather or make a miracle happen, but he can find a better outcome most of the time. They discovered it when he was very young, and his favorite toy top was washed down a disposal channel. He hummed a tune and moved his little fingers and a rock fell into the water stopping the top making it possible for his father to fish it out for him. The finder part of his gift works easily too and allows him to find all sorts of things.

Kick and Drusey are sparing different partners... yet again, but near each other. Kick is showing off and lands a devastating round-house. His girl decides she'll help his opponent Kino for fun. As Kick recovers from the blow, she playfully pushes him. This sets him off balance and allows Kino to land a superb back-kick spin hook combination. Kick is unhurt since both he and Kino are adept at pulling the power of their blows and jabs to not seriously harm the other. Kick quips, "You little minx!"

Kick stands and is promptly knocked to the ground as another trainee screams, "Run!" and hits him as he dashes by. This time, Kino and Drusey both help him to his feet. They twist in circles and glance around at their teachers who they call Commanders. The Commanders usually line the outside of The Pit to examine each sparring match and offer appropriate remediation.

"Something is wrong!" Kick exclaims. Students are running amok. He watches as the Commanders on the wall point toward the castle yelling. They are trying to drive their students away from the castle. Kick hears them shouting, "Run!"

Drusey, Kino, and Kick are experienced. They can help if they can find the source of the disruption. They seek the cause of the trouble and watch as the impossible happens. Creatures of every shape and design are pouring over the walls into The Pit. They all seem to be made of wood even though they appear in different shapes they move together, and strangely, like a puppet master is controlling them.

Kick is trying to follow the orders of the Commanders, but they are issuing conflicting orders. Some are ordering a retreat, others ordering an attack. Still, others trying to set up odd defenses.

Kick begins to move his classmates around through cover to find a way out. The Commanders are fighting trying to delay the creatures. He watches as a bolt of fire and lightning slams into one of the female Commanders. She's vaporized. They watch in shock, unsure of what to do next.

The fight is terrible for the Guild. The creatures they're fighting are easy to destroy but their numbers... there are so many of them. The intruders overwhelm a Ceorfan warrior and carry him away before any other students can help. More light flashes, a loud boom another female pupil vaporized. It looks like, as strong as the Ceorfan are, they're going to lose this fight. Kick hears the sound of another boom. Thankfully he doesn't have to see the flash and watch another sister die because he is dodging himself. The group attacking them outnumbers them by at least thirty to one.

Kick is ripping and tearing the creatures apart. Kino and Drusey are fighting hard. They battle with such fury it makes Kick believe they actually have a chance.

"Come on, guys. Let's clean up this group then get that piece of shit mage on the wall!" Kick spots the enemy mage watching him. Time slows. The evil mage's stone staff is raised and fire and lightning shoots from the staff. Kick is pushed... his beloved shoves him aside. The bolt hits Drusey straight in the chest. Kick's beautiful girl, who is standing beside him, burst into pieces... her blood spray covers him.

His heart stops! Did he just lose his Fighter? Unable to believe his eyes, he is not able to do anything but drop to his knees. The shock of losing his girl removes his desire to live.

Kino lands on Kick pushing him into the dust while trying to avoid being hit himself. Guilt fills him... "It should have been me!" he yells into the storm of creatures. "It should have been me! She pushed me out of the way."

He's devastated. There's nothing of her to save. Worse he tastes her blood on his lips. It covers his entire body, face, hair, even his hands. He quickly crawls to the walls of the arena for a safe place to shelter as he decides on a plan. Nothing makes sense. His body shaking, his life will never be the same. *She said she would be my wife, she is my everything, and now... is that all gone?* He's bouncing back and forth from reality to hell. *We didn't even have time to tell her parents she had said yes.* His heart hardens against his enemies. Before he falls, he'll kill as many of them as possible before he goes down. He doesn't want to live without her. *Fuck that! I have friends on the field of battle. I might be able to save a few of them.* He roars defiance.

His friend moves up beside him and slides behind the wall where Kick is laying. Kino must have gotten to the barrier wall just seconds after Kick did, but it feels like minutes. Hell, it seems like hours. Kick's heart turns cold in his chest. Booms blast! Time slows for him the way he was taught it does in high adrenaline situations. He didn't believe that until now.

Kick wants to tell Kino what he just saw happen to Drusey, but there's no time, one of the creatures, a massive wooden thing that looks like a gargoyle warrior raises his arms and is about to bash his friend over the head with a shield. These things are something new. They have arms and legs and move fast, but they're stupid and easy to destroy. If there weren't so many of the enemy this fight would be over minutes.

Kick raises his practice sword and hits the monster with all his anger deflecting the hit to Kino. The monster splinters with the strike and falls to the ground, unmoving. "Well, that's one down," he sneers. Kino looks at his friend and helps him up off the field. They take off for the fray in the middle of the arena finding thousands of the wooden warriors. The wooden invaders are beating the Ceorfan warriors. When one of the enemies is defeated, there are uncounted more to take its place. The warrior trainees and teaching commanders are just not enough to triumph in this battle. This time it's best to use magic to get out of here.

The school frowns on anyone using magic to get out of a fight, but this is one enemy and battle which doesn't seem to fit any rules. It's a time to save themselves and ask questions later. He's going to kill them all. The enemy is covering the Ceorfan Guild like ants on sugar. Kick's preparing with Kino's support to spell the monsters with flame.

The last thing that goes through his mind is... if he dies, good! He'll be with his love, then it's blackness.

When he wakes, the smell is overpowering. How could he have slept with that horrid odor around him is his first thought? It smells like... death.

4

PAIN AND GRIEF

ONE SECOND AFTER WAKING... A FLASH OF LIGHT AND ANOTHER boom. However, it's only in his head, his head throbs. The pain ravages Kick's body as if he were run over by the minotaur of the labyrinth. He experimentally moves his fingers. They seem to work, except for a deep dull pain letting him know what's in store as he moves the rest of his body. His body aches and shakes as he drags his way up onto an elbow to get up... *well, that hurts!*

There is part of Kick, right now, who knows what has happened. Though, he's choosing to pretend he doesn't know. He decides to live in the short term and tells himself lies to make it to the next second.

"Fat bit of good it does though!" Kick emphatically exclaims, too loudly, as he painfully rolls onto his knees. The blackness before him is so deep he can't see the difference between his eyes being open or closed. He forces his eyes as far open as he can, then rotates his head. "Nothing! I see nothing!" he says again too loudly for the situation.

Thirteen seconds after waking... The recognition of his surroundings begins to take hold. The room is quiet, warm, and it stinks. Yes, he recognizes the putrid smell of death that fills his nose. It's overpowering him, and he begins to retch. *Great, more disgust for the squalor.* Kick sings himself a song of soothing. His mind relaxes to the fear and death surrounding him.

Nineteen seconds after waking... It's time to get to work. Kick begins by tearing strips of cloth from his robe to cover his face.

Twenty-five seconds after waking... He stalls as the recognition of Drusey's death explodes from his mind and cripples his body. The sob, when it comes, is full of desperation, pain, and anger threatening to pound his mind into dust. "Drusey! Where are you Drusey!" Kick cries.

Even after remembering what he saw. His loss! Disbelief continues to cause confusion in the torn remnants of his mind. "What is going on?" he speaks aloud. Her blood spray the only remnants he has of her. Kick can't bring himself to embrace the truth of what his eyes saw. He mustn't believe it. *If I can find her, then, I know, I can save her, rescue her. That'll work. Yes... No, no, no the blood... it can't work.*

Sobbing he sits back and lets the heavy tears, and indescribable suffering be carried off into the darkness. Kick forces all of his anger to rise then blends the pain of losing her with hatred required to destroy his enemy. He vows to kill the master of the stone staff by his own hand. It doesn't matter how long it takes or what he sacrifices, he will annihilate his enemy.

Kick is spent, but now he has a mission. Now is the time to start building the tools needed to vanquish this foe. At least for now, he chooses to live. He begins by singing a spell, and his left hand becomes a glowing torch, a light in the inky dark. He needs to know if there's a way out of this prison and to see if any of these bodies around him are alive, or if they are all dead. None of them are moving.

Kick touches each individual trapped in this hell with him, gargoyle, fae, and human. A few are alive, most are not. Of the scant who are still breathing, Kick thinks he can help some but not all of them. *Better try to save them.* Gah it's so bad, he isn't sure how they will even be able to live in this filth. He doesn't know how long they've been here either, it's been long enough that he knows he's hungry. His stomach growls. He doesn't care. Caring would mean to crave life. He doesn't. He does desire revenge.

Kick searches the dank room. Again, bile rises in his throat at the revelation of each new horror in front of him. He finally finds his friend Kino. He feels for a pulse. *He's alive, thank the Creator, I'm not alone!* Kick tries to wake his friend. He doesn't stir. Kick pulls his gargoyle friend to an area of the room which isn't as squalid and realizes he still cares about something. He must save his friend.

Kick begins sorting the dead from the living, piling them as respectfully as possible along the foulest parts of the far wall. He moves the living to the opposite wall, laying them along the least repellant wall, farthest from the slain, with their knees toward their chests. Kick apologizes to each of the dead as he removes any article of clothing which is semi-clean or can be used as bandages. He tears them into strips and binds all the wounds on the unconscious. This is Kick operating on automatic. It's what he does—care for people. He does this in spite of his hardened heart. His reflexes know that his hardness is explicitly reserved for his enemy. The one with the fire shooting staff.

He sits and hums to himself for a few minutes to collect himself, then resolves to get busy again.

5

IN PRISON

SOMETHING TOUCHES KICK'S ARM. IN HIS SHOCK, HE reflexively jumps while letting out an audible grunt and clutches the individual he is carrying. The warrior mage holds his glowing fingers out and sees Kino squatting beside him.

Kino says, "Let me help. Do you recognize where we are, Kick? Are you uninjured?"

Kick grabs his friend in a hug. They both stifle tears.

"Fuck! I'm fine. I was just startled, I thought that one of the dead touched me," Kick gasps. "Several have moved, and no, I don't have a clue where we are. There have been no noises I haven't made or any smell I can register except for the deceased. No one is here to ask anything. Kino, do you know what happened to Drusey?"

"Yes, I am sorry, my friend. What do you want me to do to help you? I will happily assist you and help make the enemy pay. In all aspects, I want them to pay. I know you saw the white-haired mage with the staff when he killed Drusey. Did you recognize him?"

Kick stops and thinks for a minute. "Now that you mention it, he could be one of the instructors at the school. Is that what you're thinking?"

Kino nods and says, "Yes that is what I am assuming. I am certain his name is Baratium Mezacain. I saw him working with the headmaster last week. I had to go to the skene to retrieve my new instrument for the musical spell class."

"At least, now I know who to kill," Kick states. "I just don't know how I'll get to him. Thank you, Kino, for caring and saying you'll help me. Destroying this piece of shit is something I'll do. Even if it takes my last breath."

"Yes, my friend. I will be with you to the end, I swear."

"Shh, I hear someone coming. Let's try to get answers. The more we learn, the faster I can kill him."

By this point, the two Ceorfan mages have placed all the dead on one side of the room and are tending to the living on the other side. Neither Kick nor Kino have a way to pretend to be still out cold. They did, however, need to pretend to be in the dark. Kick quickly extinguishes the light from his hand and they both stand with the living, waiting to see if their jailers will come into the cell.

The door is thick and strong as they push it open. Kick can see the door houses a small window about the size of a square dinner plate with a covering over it. He also notices, to his regret, the large door doesn't have a handle on their side. He watches it roughly scuff along the floor as it opens. Several of the wooden monsters enter in front of a tall mage and a much younger, smaller man. Kick assumes the tall one is a mage because of his dress. The older of the two has long stringy, straight, hair braided into long ropey strands. The brownish-red of his younger years still staining the greying almost matted hairstyle. The younger man stands back, out of the way, watching. *The younger guy must be his assistant or apprentice probably a mage also.*

The rusty-haired mage points an arthritic looking finger toward the fallen. Ordering, by some unknown means, the monsters to remove them from the room. He's a wiry man who looks as if he doesn't eat, maybe. Despite the grey touching throughout his goatee beard, his green-gold eyes are full of energy. They dance from one target to another. Cold and cunning, yet not crazy. His tan is so dark it appears to reflect his soul. It's evident that years in the sun have also taken their toll making his skin appear leathery and wrinkled. In the broadest and possibly strangest sense, you could consider him handsome. If you like bespectacled wrinkled arthritic old mass murderers that is.

His creepy darker haired assistant remains in the shadows, listening and waiting. *Waiting for what I wonder? Is he the loyal protector, bracing to strike in a moment's notice?* As the monsters begin the grim task of cleaning out the deceased, the ancient wizard stops two of them and directs them to transfer two of the murdered to his laboratory... for experimental purposes he says. Kick and Kino silently fume. Still, they both agree this isn't the time to start a fight or any action.

The removal of the lifeless bodies does nothing for the stench in the cell. The grizzled mage turns his regard toward Kick and Kino. As he turns, Kick sees the other side of his face. It has, what looks to be a magical brand of a horned, winged serpent. The winged snake seems to move as Kick watches.

The old mage looks directly at the Ceorfan men, peering into their eyes. Speaking to a spot nearer Kick, but including Kino, he tells them, "Don't bother with your magic. I've locked you away from it. If you ever had any to begin with!" He cackles.

"You two, out of the chamber!" he orders pointing at the Ceorfan warrior mages. When they're standing in a hall outside of the cell, his assistant closes and locks the door. Kick shivers inwardly. *This is a bad sign.*

The remaining monsters take hold of the young Ceorfan in vice-like grips and haul them down the slimy hallway. It soon becomes plain they're in an underground prison. It's dark, wet, and the further down they move, cool. They've been moving in random directions up, down, left, right ostensibly to keep them from being able to retrace their steps. They arrive in a broad vacant area they could consider 'nicer' than the chamber they woke up in. Still, they both recognize it for what it is, a dungeon.

Several smaller cells line the room on opposite sides. A few of the places are larger and ready to contain more captives than most of the other units. As they are being led toward the cells, Kick asks, "What'll happen to our companions in the other cell? Will their wounds be tended too?" A slap in the head by one of the wooden beasts is Kick's reward for speaking.

With the tiniest of glances to Kino, Kick makes his plan known. Well, not his plan per se. But his friend knows that he is about to attack so stumbles and falls hard into the monster in front of him. As he does, Kick launches himself at the two closest animals, landing devastating kicks to both, sending shards of wood flying in all angles. Kino continues his fall onto the wooden machine. As one hits the ground, he rolls over its head, his red locks flying and grabs its arms then with scant effort tears them off. He then uses the pieces as a club to beat his victim to splinters.

The two prisoners are quickly on their feet and ready themselves when three more come toward the redheaded Ceorfan mage and four more toward his friend. The two hopeful escapees turn to attack. Their former Commanders would compliment the grace with which they move together... if they were still alive. However, within a few seconds, each has taken out another of the brutes. Someone grabs them from behind, and they turn to face their next opponent.

Kino's reward for being recaptured is being smashed in the head. As he falls, several of the animals set upon him, beating him without mercy.

Kick is still struggling, trying to free himself from the grasp of the beast, when a second one grabs one of his arms, yet another grabs his other arm. A fourth pounds him from the front.

More of the vile creations pour into the room ensuring there's no further struggle, and that they beat both prisoners into submission.

They shove the Ceorfan into separate compartments. Kick groans in pain and tries to talk to Kino through a swelling face, bloody mouth, and bruised ribs. He'd bitten his tongue when they surprised him with the first fist to the face when he asks about his friends in the other cell. Kino isn't answering. He must be unconscious again.

Weakened from his previous beating, Kick rolls gingerly onto his side. The cold of the floor feels good to his bruised face and body. Laying there he wonders why he's able to remain conscious, or at least regain awareness faster, while Kino can't. *Is it my magic making me strong? But, didn't the murderous old shitbag tell us he had locked away our magic? I know it can't be true for me; I used my hand like a torch and I'm able to remain conscious when all the others can't.*

Kick tries singing a little spell to heal Kino. He sings the healing song as low as he can, so he doesn't call attention to himself or to Kino.

His friend moans then croaks, "The spell is working, thank you."

They talk in low tones. "Kino, I want to fight again the next time they open our cells. I won't quit fighting. I don't fear death and don't worry about giving up."

"I agree with you. I also believe this old mage will kill us when it suits him."

"Kino, I still have magic. Do you understand what that means?"

"Yes, it means the old goat was wrong about having it locked away."

"You try. Try singing a spell to help heal me."

"Okay," Kino sings. Nothing happens. Kino doesn't have access to any of his magic.

"What does it mean, Kino? Why would I be able to use it and not you?"

"I believe it may be because you are part fae."

"Okay, so I'll fight this time, and you watch to see what happens. Maybe, we can get some idea of how to attack these monsters."

"Agreed," Kino answered.

They each have a small cot and a bucket of water in their cells.

They clean up using a scrap of cloth torn from their clothes. When they rest, it's done in shifts so one can rest while the other watches for the guards. It's not an easy way to sleep, but when they get the chance, their soldier training tells them to make it happen to be healthy enough to keep fighting.

6

THEY FIGHT

Kick and Kino wake after a few hours of sleep each. Their recent beating has left them both sore and swollen. Kino isn't worried. In a few hours, the sun will set, and he'll torpify, harden to stone, and fully heal.

They hear the guards walking down the hall toward their door.

"Kino, get ready. If they open a cell, we need to be ready to break free. The old mage is our target. We need to kill that fucker as fast as we can."

"I agree, my friend. To rescue the others, I believe we must kill the mage. Just to have a chance..."

The footsteps stop in front of their cells' barred doors. Keys rattle, and one of their captors opens Kick's door then Kino's. The doors scuff their way open. They see the monsters first. When the first of the wooden demons enter the room, Kick sees the mage who held the crystal stone staff. He freezes. He pays little attention to the other monsters or the wretched old rusty-gray headed mage entering behind Baratium. Kick is focused on Baratium... *Hold on a second, what's the thing he's carrying...* The next moment a wooden beast is moving something... a figure, unrecognizable to either prisoner.

Baratium sneers at the Ceorfan mages then slightly almost imperceptibly deepens his smirk. If Baratium notices the smell in the area, he pays it no attention. He steps toward Kino's cell drawing all eyes to him and away from the body being held by the creature. Looking directly at Kino, he states, "Ceorfan Guild prisoners, I need information. You have a choice to make. Either give me, the information I require... or watch someone you love die." Baratium pauses and doesn't waver as he stares in Kino's direction.

Despite the intended intimidation, Kino's answer is swift and unambiguous, "I will not assist you."

The old, skinny mage moves in and unlocks Kino's cell. "You will," Baratium said assuredly. "I will give you this single chance. Provide me the information I require regarding the Ceorfan queen's men, including their locations. I'll provide you the maps to use with which to do so."

As if already torpified, Kino doesn't move or speak.

"The next thing I'll do is a warning to you and you," the murderer says pointing at them both in turn. He twists around to signal to his assistant. "Walter, get me my information and provide me a larger army," Baratium orders then leaves the room.

Walter laughs, "My master may want this done as a warning." He looks around with glee on his leathery face. "I'm doing it because I enjoy it." He adds a cackle for extra creepiness. Walter points a boney finger, again functioning as a command to the wooden thing holding the body. The wooden killers move out of the shadows and into the light. They drop the body. It unfolds like a rolled-up rug, plummeting toward the ground. Only instead of hitting the ground hard, its held arms jerk the body to a stop. Now hanging before them is Kino's father, Feodras, hoisted aloft by his wrists.

"Father!" Kino exclaims.

"Do not tell the queen's secrets, son," Feodras demands. A tone Kino knows well from living with his father. A tone he knows means, 'I would rather die than dishonor or show disloyalty to my queen.'

For his words, Feodras is punched once, twice, then pounded and eventually dropped to the ground, kicked, and beaten by the four beasts. All the while Walter laughs.

"Wait! Please stop. You're killing him... please." Kino pushes open his cell door and throws his body on top of the father, using his body to protect his father's. When that doesn't seem like enough, Kino folds his wings over and around him. He's stopped. Apparently, Walter has some powerful magic too, and he uses it to freeze Kino. Kick was watching his friend and missed the magic that is used against him. *How did Walter freeze him so completely? Nothing is moving except the panting of his chest. He isn't even moving his eyes or eyelids. Was it Walter or the creepy bastard?*

Walter makes the wooden beasts open another cell. Kino's dad is too beat up to fight or to even break his own fall as he's thrown unceremoniously into the back wall before he crashes to the floor. Feodras lies on the floor, unmoving.

Walter cackles again as he points to Kino and says, "You, come with me to be carved it's close to sunrise, and my master needs many pieces of you to make more soldiers."

Kick panicking, yells, "Wait what do you mean you will carve him? You can't... No! Wait!"

Kick continues to plead to save his friend. Walter seems to enjoy the extra misery this is adding. The wooden demons pick Kino up and take him to the old mage's lab. There, they set his feet in a washtub and stand his pain ridden and frozen body there.

7

TORPED HEALING

It's not widely known, even among the Ceorfan, that there's a process called Resurgere. It's a dangerous undertaking that they can use to make gargoyles. During the ceremony, they cut a piece of a gargoyle flesh from a living gargoyle. Simultaneously, a portion of bone is cut from a person, alive or dead. The gargoyle tissue is placed inside the human, and they set the bone into the gargoyle. If the human is dead, it restores the person to life as a gargoyle. In all cases, the process makes the gargoyle and human into a family—for as long as they live. It's not done often because it has sometimes backfired with disastrous results. The created 'Carved' gargoyles have, depending on the character of the person, become hateful beings incapable of love. They don't cherish peace and refuse to act as protectors of the world or the Ceorfan Guild. Instead, they're bent only on destruction.

"You shall stay stiffened, so I don't have a problem carving your flesh to make my master's Crafted. That is what I call my creations. Do you think they are beautiful? The ones who overtook your whole Ceorfan army while they were already in fighting gear," the old mage gloats.

Kino can't say anything and worries more for his father than for himself. He realizes that if the old mage performs a type of Resurgere; he'll father some of these hateful wooden creatures. *Maybe, if I pour all of my love, all of my compassion into my body, they will get some of my thoughts and not be as tied to evil. What is the chance they will help us overcome our captors, and we can escape?* This is how Kino thinks, always calculating the best outcome in any situation.

When Walter makes the first cut, Kino doesn't quite understand what is happening. The pressure and burning aren't what he was expecting. That first cut slices into his lower back. Kino strains to relax and meditate to keep the pain from taking his wits.

The next cut is near the first. Again, pressure and burning. The combined pain growing in intensity. Almost as if a torch were being held near his lower back.

Kino feels the blood as it runs down his back and leg and onto his foot. As he notices the blood, panic rips his mind. He watches Walter take an iron from the fire. The metal is glowing orange and carries the flame from the fire with it as it moves toward him. The old codger touches the torch to his open wounds and burns the exposed flesh. Pain overtakes Kino's defenses and forces him to question how much longer he has to live, how much longer he even wants to live. The smell of burning flesh invades his senses as his lungs fill with the vile stench. He suffers the next slice, then again, the pressure and the cauterization making him quiver in pain.

"Oh, how inimical of me," Walter says. "If I cut you like this, you should know what tools I use. To cut you, I'm using this rounded diamond scalpel. You know, you should be grateful that I use a sharp instrument. The dull ones hurt far more." Kino gasps at more pressure and the burning born of the cutting. He also endures the onset of shock. "After I remove the chunk of flesh I want..." Kino observes the pull on his back and the pressure and pain as it's cut free. "... I must stop the bleeding. To do so, I use this." He removes the bright orange rod from the brazier. He pauses with the hot metal, so Kino can see it and can appreciate what is happening to him. Then moves behind the gargoyle's back. The bloom of pain from this third application is more than Kino can handle, and he begins to black out. The pain is horrifying. He reels from each new cut, each cauterization of his flesh. Cut after cut, burn after burn, he fights for his freedom. He tries to scream. He can't yell, only breathe and gasp air. When the torch is applied, his impulse is to flinch away from the burning terror. Yet, the only external movement the spell allows his body is his chest expanding and contracting, expelling and refilling his lungs. Even that is torture as it sucks in the putrid burning flesh, refilling his lungs each time with even more burnt pieces of himself. The shock of the three agonies leaves him screaming for relief in his own mind. Kino is glad that the old mage has frozen him stiff. Otherwise, he would thrash around and be cut worse. Frozen or not, his tears flow.

The old mage croons, "Come come, you are a mighty Ceorfan warrior. This is for a good cause, we will take the world from the humans before they ruin it. Think of all the good your body is creating for us. For every one of the Crafted, you make from being carved you contribute to killing some of the human scum. Baratium will love you and make you a general in his army if you swear fealty to him."

Not on any terms!

Baratium became his mortal enemy for life the minute he invaded the arena. Kino will fight tomorrow if they try this again. He exalts in the familiar tingle of sunrise and the extra pain caused by the torpification process mixes with the torture caused by Walter. His body takes the combined pain, just for a few seconds while he hardens to stone and slips into sleep. He changed to beautiful red marble to be exact. Kino is a beauty of a gargoyle that can't be denied. His muscular body is larger than most, his wings folded against his body isn't normal for him; he poses with them up and extended when he sleeps. The pain on his face is hardened in place, his horns flow back from his head gleaming in the room's light.

Now that the vicious old mage has enough flesh made stone nuggets he puts them into wooden statues he's prepared for this purpose. He chants the spells the entire time, making more of the Crafted demons come to life—of sorts. Yet, these are only robots and will do as someone tells them or nothing. He motions with one hand for them to line up against the wall like the terra cotta warriors awaiting their emperor.

Walter remembers that Kino needs to be locked back in his cell before his torpification, or hardening, is over and he becomes flesh again. So, he tells his Crafted slaves to take him to his cell. When they do, they set him in and leave not caring about the other prisoners or what they're doing.

8

THE OTHERS HERE

Kick wakes up when they bring Kino back into his cell. Not knowing whether it's safe to be awake, he pretends he's not. During the day, he fell asleep without meaning to; he needs it. When he wakes, he hears voices. Unmoving he tries to gather a little information before anyone knows he's aware. Shocked, he figures out the other cells are full. *When did that happen?* It's the other mages who were taken prisoner when he was. Glad on one hand they're out of the dank chamber and survived, upset they are caged. He moves so he can see and yes, all the cells are packed. The larger units have several Ceorfan mages in each. They're talking without caring who hears them.

Getting up Kick inspects his surroundings. These are his fellow students from the Warrior Mage School, the teaching facility for any gifted one who wants to learn. Most mages want to learn more about magic and how to better control theirs. So, do most parents of the magic born. It's rare that a spell user doesn't attend this school, regardless of their station in life.

The queen of the Ceorfan wants everyone to have a chance at an education. She has commissioned several schools specializing in various arts and sciences. The mage school is only one. The gargoyle queen plans for more but they have schools for cooks, warriors, historians... and more. No one is excluded, not only gargoyles who are the primary population of the Ceorfan, but humans, fae, sea people— everyone is welcome. That's how the Ceorfan work, they try to help others. Still, most of those who attend are those rejected by society who become part of the Ceorfan people.

Peter, one of the younger and more talented mages notices Kick's eyes are open. He says, "Hey there, I was wondering when you would wake. They have left us food and water. Yours they put in the far corner as you slept. It's only bread, and not too old. It's better than I thought they'd give us. Eat, and we'll tell you what we've found out so far."

Kick nods at his blonde classmate and gathers the food. He eats while Peter tells him what they've discovered. "The monsters are ignorant and don't respond to questions or touch. They show up, do what they're told, and leave. I also think we're underground because of the cold damp conditions. He motions to one of the others. "Slade thinks because he's fae it explains why his magic works when no one else's is functioning. That's all we've got. Have you been able to learn anything more?"

Kick says, "Well-being fae is good reasoning. I'm half fae and half human and my magic functions and Kino's doesn't. We've figured out the evil mage who started this war is Baratium Mezacain. He's brought us here with his two minions, Walter is the creep with rusty colored gray hair. Rusty-creep is most likely human. The other one is Walter's assistant or apprentice. One of them can freeze a person, so they can't move a muscle. The ass is heartless. He had the wood demons beat Kino's dad, Feodras, within an inch of his life. Then they threw him into the cell across from his son." Everyone looks toward the torped gargoyles and stops to concentrate for a few seconds. Sunset is soon. They sense it. Steen suggests, "When it's time, absorb as much magic from the shift of the gargoyles as you can. It may help us."

During their shifting there's magic in the air. The mages have learned to gather the energy. The process is beginning. Invisible zaps tingle on their skin for a second, then a sound similar to breaking glass crackles, and the gargoyles are once again free. There are only five, and they are all in the cells with Kino and Feodras.

Kino comes forward and asks, "Is it safe to speak?"

His body is restored and there isn't a mark on him. His mind though is fighting the panic from the horror of last night. Several of the prisoners answer him it's safe and the monsters pay no attention to them.

"Father, are you all right now? I'm so sorry I wasn't capable of defending you last night," Kino cries.

Feodras responds, "I know that son. I am revived. Do not worry about me. I understand you did what you could. But how are *you*, my son? What happened to you last night?"

Kino continues, "It was a living nightmare! They took me to the evil old mage's laboratory. The devils are called Crafted by their master. They are made from us in a Resurgere type spell." Several groans. "When they took me, the bastard cut me so many times it was either torp fast or die."

Kick says, "That explains why we're here. It seems, gentlemen, that this evil old human needs us to create more Crafted for his army. They want the mages for our magic and the gargoyles for their bodies. The question is... how do we escape and not help them in the meantime?"

Kino answers, "I had no choice. That manic pig, Walter, had me frozen by his young assistant. If they come for me again, I plan to resist and rush him before he can spell me. If nothing else I can kill at least one of our captors. Do any of you have enough magic to shield me while I try?"

At this, the prisoners sit and plan for their day. When they catch the echo of footsteps they quiet.

9

THEY LEARN TO OBEY

THE PRISONERS SIT MUTE AND UNMOVING IN THEIR CELLS. Souls paralyzed not by magic or fear, but the realization of facing a threat unlike any they have ever faced before. Their faces are transfixed on Baratium as he approaches. He is tall and sturdy looking with his bloody magic staff in his hand. A look of superiority and malice is stamped on his face. That staff... is the one he used to kill Drusey. In that minute, Kick imagines the great glee he'll receive in destroying this vile fuck.

The mage who had committed the horrid monstrous acts can't be considered handsome by any normal definition, he isn't. His ugly isn't skin deep. It permeates through his entire existence. However, there's an underlying appeal. He projects raw power which those who hate him most can perceive. The condescending sneer on his face for his captives shows the pure disgust he feels for Ceorfan, even though they're in his jail, under his control. It is Baratium's opinion that the Ceorfan are nothing but rejects, imbeciles who should have been killed at birth. The truth of those views shows in his body language. With him today are Crafted and the ancient Walter, who tortured

Kino. He struts up the aisle of the dungeon then takes a profound breath to begin his speech.

"My name is Baratium. For too long we've lived with the human scum fouling this planet and their chaos of subjugating those who should be their rulers. The humans act as lords of the races and relegate the true masters to extinction. I will take their power. Power that is mine by right. I guarantee to employ it with restraint to anyone who will swear fealty at my feet," he proposes. There's a beat, a melody matching the tone of his voice. It's almost captivating and draws the consideration of those in the dungeon. Although, he's a narcissistic psychopath he seems to have gotten the rapt attention of everyone. It's a spell. He's trying to add us to his forces. It won't work, but he can try.

The murderer continues, "My army and I struck the first blow for justice early this morning. As of that time forward, I became your master. To those who prefer to oppose me. The consequences of your choice will be devastating. Make no mistake, the decision is yours. But understand this, most of you will not live through them, so don't force my hand. This proposal is the only occasion I'll offer. I require a larger army. Those of you who are gargoyles will do this for me and make my army bigger, without argument. If you ignore my goodwill, I'll ensure you will live to regret it." He actually smiles a half grin.

"Those of you who have magic will be included in learning the process of creating my army. I have now offered my terms and warned you of the results if you do not live up to them. Who of you elect to defy me?"

"Defy you? No, I won't defy you. I rebuke you. I repudiate every word that has exited that pie-hole in your face," Slade spits out.

Kick evaluates the situation to back up his fellow prisoner. Baratium's bemused expression is all that's required to recognize what he is doing. "Shit, shit, shit," Kick whispers in rapid fire. "It's a test... don't fall for it. Slade, shut up... please just shut the fuck up!" Kick begs. Then he becomes still, examining every detail of their jailer's mercy. Unsure of who will help, the young Ceorfan mage holds back. His only hope is to gain every speck of knowledge he can to use in overcoming this micro-phallic ass when the proper time comes.

Baratium motions for Slade to come forward. The enthusiastic Slade moves to the front of the cell. Their captor moves a finger and the door swings open. Dread in the place is palpable. Kick prays for Slade to fall at the mage's feet and swear fealty, so he can live to fight another day. Slade walks through the exit. Kick prepares to move.

Baratium points his crystal staff at Slade and white-hot lightning blasts from it hitting Slade in the chest. On contact Slade explodes. In less than a whisper of a second, it's over. The spray of blood and gore cover the hostages. They back away from the psychopath. At the onset of the murder they moved as far away as they can, several try to climb the wall. Kick is stunned.

"Such a tragedy to lose a student so young. I feel no amusement in the loss," Baratium states. Kick detects a smile though. Which tells him the ass enjoyed it a lot. But like all despots he'll claim to be a man of the people fighting a greater enemy, yet will destroy any who defy him.

"I implore you. Do what I say and don't challenge me. I will win. Do you need me to provide another example?" the crazed madman asks. Turning to his servant he orders, "Walter, get the prisoners cleaned up and clean these cells too. This stink is oppressing." With his robes flowing wide as he exits two of the Crafted follow him providing a silent guard. With that, he's out of their sight.

The old reprobate nods his head at his master's back and responds, "Yes, master." No other words.

Walter swiveling his chicken neck twists around and chides the captives. "He says he'll do it and he does. Learn what I will teach you and obey. Now, remove your clothes. They offend our master."

The prisoners strip. Wooden devils collect the bloody clothes for disposal. Since the cells don't have drains in the floor, the rusty old creep orders the Crafted to herd them into a nearby washing room. Walter doesn't even try to cover his ogling of their fine bodies when they are ordered to bathe—needless to say, the shower is a gift. The

Ceorfan want to remove the sweat, the blood, and the gore from the battle and from Slade's recent destruction. They're given soap to use under a waterfall of lukewarm water. Each prisoner shares the shower with two or three of his fellow hostages.

Kick washes himself because he wishes to wash the pain and bile of the day from his body, as a promise of washing it from his mind. Yet as he watches, as the blood runs off of his body and onto the floor, he has a moment of anguish... Kick cries. He uses the flow of the waterfall to cover his tears. He realizes the last he'll ever see of his love is that very blood now flowing down the drain. His Drusey is now gone. He fights the urge to fall to his knees and save some of her. There is no way to save even a piece of her, it's futile.

Now clean they are herded back to their cells. While they were out, Walter ordered the Crafted to scrub the cells and dungeon rooms that are their prison. Now back, the captives aren't provided a stitch of clothing. If the horrid old mage believes this will hurt them he doesn't understand Ceorfan. Clothes are an option for gargoyles. They don't get hot or cold, and above all they are all soldiers. The Guild doesn't care about nudity. They care about getting out of here, so they spend most of the rest of the night planning their escape.

10

IT'S ALL DEATH

RIGHT BEFORE SUNRISE, THE ANCIENT MAGE, WALTER, COMES to force them to do as Baratium has demanded—produce more Crafted.

Feodras and Kino were both near the door when Walter approaches. He instructs them to backup, and they comply. Walter opens Feodras' cell. A large Crafted moves in and secures him. Walter goes to Kino's cell next, he had moved away from his cell door when he was ordered with Feodras. Kino now stands what looks like a good distance away from the door. Kick and every other Ceorfan knows the door is still only a single long stride away for the big red gargoyle.

Walter slides the key in the lock. Kino drops his hips to prepare. The door opens. In a flash of red, with white claws and teeth, Kino rushes Walter. He drops him before anyone can react. Kino lands on Walter and has his hands around his throat. The red goyle is about to snap his neck. As Kino springs, Walter's young apprentice acts almost as fast, freezing Kino again. But this time, with Kino's hands frozen around the old psychopath's neck. Given the red goyle's immobile hands around his neck, Walter isn't able to move from Kino's grasp.

In a tone reminiscent of a mallard's honk Walter demands, "Crafted, remove one of this filthy guano eater's hands." His raspy voice runs out of power as he spits out the command with a cough. The closest Crafted cuts the meat of Kino's arm completing a grisly band around his wrist. Then in a sickening sight, the monster brings a giant arm down and in a loud, "crack," breaks the bones. Kino's hand falls to the floor with a sickening splat. This process takes only seconds and leaves the room in utter silence. The sharp knife cut and the subsequent spray of blood cover Walter and the Crafted that did the cutting.

Walter scrambles out of the way reaching into his robes, he removes a stone from his pocket. Then chanting a strange spell, the rusty old mage uses the stone to cauterize Kino's severed wrist, ending the spray of blood. Walter picks up the amputated hand and turns facing the other prisoners. He wheezes, "Our Master has been generous to you. Even to you." Pointing at the paralyzed Kino with his own hand. "He didn't want this war. They forced it upon him by the less worthy. He could have destroyed all of you. Yet he didn't, and this is the gratitude you offer. There must be a lesson! Gargoyles you are little more than pond scum, anyway. Therefore, this lesson will be marvelous in its implementation. Still using Kino's severed body part, he points at Feodras while peering at Kino. "This is your parent is it not?" The feral smile on Walter's face tells them the only thing they need to know about how he intends to handle the gargoyles. Showing them all he will take great pleasure in the action, Walter orders the Crafted, "Kill the father!" Four Crafted take hold of each of his limbs and a fifth, his head. One by one, they dismember him, saving his screaming head for last. There's no coming back from this kind of death, gargoyle or no. Kino is still and can't move. His silent screams only heard in his own private terrifying existence. In his paralyzed state he watches the pieces of the man he loves drop to the floor. He vows revenge. *Goodbye father, you were my first and best friend*. The other prisoners stand horrified, sorrow, and defiance prevalent on their faces. If they weren't previously knit together in a cause, they are now. Kick is furious, hanging onto his rage by a thread.

He commands, "Walter, fix Kino's hand."

The old psycho asks, "Or, what will you do?" His voice is whiny and insolent.

Kick thinks, then answers, "I'll make you a deal. I'll go without a fight and do what you require if you put his hand back on before he torps, so it can heal."

"It is a deal then... apprentice." The old goat cackles.

Kick is glad that the hand will be reattached but upset he has become the apprentice of the vile evil Walter. Kick's always looking for any angle to work. Here, he has no choice. Becoming one of Walter's apprentices might just get him—all of them—some freedom they need to figure out how to escape. The others are as compliant as he is as they take them from their cells. They step over the pieces of their old master Feodras as they are led to the laboratory.

Upon reaching the workshop Kick asks, "What are you expecting us to call you, old man?"

"From this day forward, I'm your Commander. You may call me Commander. My name is Walter Deveros, and you may call me by either name. Your master Baratium you will call, Master. My assistant is Bladriell. So, my new apprentice, what is your name?"

Kick says coolly, "Gortanik Lonato." He is unwilling to call Walter—Commander or give him his nickname. *That name is only for friends.*

Walter lets him get away with the minor insult. "The Crafted don't have names they only respond to the one who controls them. That magic spell is for the Master and me. Remember that or I'll bring in more of your loved ones." He removes an amulet from his robes and places it around his neck and chants his spell, "Great Lord Thoth, open your cistern, restore the magic to these beasts." That simple incantation restores the magic of the Ceorfan students. No one notices a difference, no sound, no light, not a feeling on their skin.

There would be no way to know there was a change if they hadn't been told.

What they do next isn't easy for any of them. In fact, they couldn't do it at all if not for what they had just witnessed with the destruction of Feodras. The now more mellow, but still psychotic Walter tests each mage for the magic they own. In his typical style, Walter warns each student, "If I find your magic lacking, or if you lie, I'll call the Crafted." Walter places extra emphasis on certain words to make his intentions clear.

Each student has the requisite powers required for the Resurgere spell which they will use to create the Crafted. Walter doesn't know Kino, being a gargoyle, is also a mage. No one tells him either.

Walter teaches the prisoners to recite the spell while he carves Kino's flesh. "From flesh there is life. From life there is motion. From motion, I create the pliant."

Blood runs in rivulets down the red goyle's immobile body pooling in the tub's bottom he's standing in. After repeating the spell several times followed by the burning flesh from the cauterization, Walter instructs the students in how to carve the gargoyles. Five gargoyle prisoners besides Kino are held in front of the Ceorfan mages. The goyles stand in their own washtubs. No one moves. There is one gargoyle to two mages one in front and one behind the containers. The mages are all given a cutter. Kick watches Peter rub the edge and cut himself and suck on the cut.

Walter trains them, "This is a diamond scalpel. You must be careful not to cut too deeply. The gargoyles must survive long enough to torpify at sunrise. Since it's only minutes away, you should be able to do this without killing them. When they have healed, we'll repeat this process. Then do it again and again until our master tells us he has a large enough army." Walter walks the room as he talks to them. He looks into each of the faces of his students ensuring they know he'll be watching them.

Walter continues by demonstrating, once again, how to cut. This time, he uses Kick as his instruction device. Only now, Kick has to cut his friend, Kino. Kick's whole body is rigid with anger. Kick holds it in and does as he's told.

This mage is dead as soon as we're free. Baratium will die first, then Walter. Right now, I have to protect our family. I can't let Baratium or Walter look for my parents, or even Kino's sister or mother. No, I'll wait for a better time, a time when I'm sure of victory. He stares into Kino's eyes hoping Kino understands the decision he is faced with and will forgive him for what he is about to do. Hopefully, Kino knows he doesn't want to hurt him. Kick prays Kino remains his friend.

"Please, forgive me, brother," Kick begs. All the mages stare at the diamond scalpel in their hands. They struggle with obeying until one gargoyle, Krag says, "Do what he wants, we'll survive and fight when it's our time."

Steen who is standing in front of him, nods and says, "Please, forgive me, Krag."

Every one of the Ceorfan repeats this plea of forgiveness to the gargoyles as they prepare to cut their friends, their fellow countrymen.

Then when sickass Walter tells them all to begin the chant with him, they do, when he says cut, they do. Blood runs down their friends, pooling in the washtubs as tears run from the mages' eyes. The students chant, "From flesh there is life. From life there is motion. From motion, I create the pliant." The gargoyles scream. They try not to show how much the pain is. None of them want Walter to see how he is hurting them. None want their friends to hear the real pain they suffer. They try to fight for decorum but fail, in this it is good that they are held steady by the Crafted. For the next few minutes, the gargoyles are cut so much that no part of their bodies remains unbloodied.

Kick can sense the sunrise nearing. He warns Walter, "Deveros! Do not forget your promise! Replace Kino's hand."

Again, Walter ignores the slight from Kick and only tilts a nod to the warrior mage. He picks up Kino's bloody appendage and replaces it on the burned stump, holding it in place with a magic field. The students feel the return of the sun and stop the cutting. As the gargoyles harden, a collective sigh of relief sounds in the room. The gargoyles can now heal. The students, examining the blood of their brothers remaining on their hands are filled with guilt.

Kick examines his friend, Kino. He sees that the hand appears to have been restored correctly. The dark-haired mage breathes a satisfied sigh as it seems he won the day if he chooses to only examine the day from this small victory. It is how his gift operates, changing things. As the only Changer-Finder, he has ever known it sometimes escapes him when a change in circumstance happens because of him but not this time. He'll see victory in a day of defeats if it leads him toward his ultimate goal. Here, keeping Kino intact as a fighter counts as a win.

The Crafted herd them back to the bathroom to shower again. This time, they wash the blood of their friends which they caused. Not a word is spoken. As they're returned to the cells, they find that the pieces of Feodras have been removed and the gargoyles have been returned to their cells. None speak of the horrors they just committed. There isn't anything to say. None of them try. One by one, they fall into a troubled sleep depleted of peace. Some cry out fighting the enemy in their uneasy rest. Some never sleep at all.

Maybe tomorrow they'll find a way to freedom.

11

KINO IS GONE

THE FIRST HORRIFYING WEEK OF CUTTING THEIR CEORFAN family ends. Kick and the others are exhausted. They are sitting in their cells and talking when the dark-haired warrior says, "Kino, I can't continue. I can't put my family in danger, but you're my family too. I can't... I won't continue to torture you every day."

"My friend, you are my brother for today and all days. I know your heart. You and the others have not chosen this path. Like mine, they have forced it on you. I also cannot abide you placing others in danger to save me from pain, no matter how torturous it is. I will survive it, or not."

Peter chimes in, "I agree with Kick, I'm fed up with hurting you all too." There's a murmur throughout the room as the other mages agree.

"Brothers, you cannot place your families at risk to save us pain. Their deaths would be on our consciences for eternity. Please do not place that burden on us," Kino says while motioning for the noise to quiet. "We cannot escape. Please let us use our spare time positively."

"Kino's right," Kick says. "We may not be able to escape, but I don't have to let that piece of shit Walter force me to keep hurting you."

"Kick, please listen...," starts the red goyle.

"No, listen. Give me a chance to explain. I have an idea. They can force me to cut you. True. You won't let me quit helping the shits. What if I can place a spell on you, so you can't feel it! I have never tried anything like this, other than a minor numbing for a small cut that needs stitched, but it's worth a try. I'm sure I can make it work!"

The room falls silent until Peter breaks it. He asks, "Kick can you teach the rest of us the spell?"

"Yeah, I'm sure I can. At a minimum, I can teach each of you to spell the area you're getting ready to cut! All right let's make plans."

Kick spends the next few hours teaching the spell to his fellow mages.

Kino spends the time ensuring that his fellow gargoyles will continue to play the role of tortured trash. Their first test proved a resounding success. Kick forges a win in what should be an unwinnable situation. He never tells Walter as a 'good' apprentice would. The dark-haired mage laughs to himself. "I guess I won't get extra credit at this apprenticeship school," he says.

The days blur, one into another. One day turns into a week which becomes months. The Ceorfan have yet to find a way out of their prison. They've fallen into a routine, each day passing much like the one before. Although the gargoyles being cut, no longer feel the pain of the carving, the knowledge that their bodies are being used to create more of Baratium's army provides great psychological distress. It's almost as unbearable.

Their cycle of pain has become routine. There are now thousands upon thousands of Crafted. Made from the unwilling but pliant captives. Day after day without interruptions or change. One day, the cell door scrapes open when it shouldn't have. Two large Crafted monsters enter the room followed by Baratium Mezacain. The place falls silent. None of the inmates move. Not out of worry for their individual safety; but more of a general malaise which has set into their jail. Kick opens his eyes wide to his friends Peter and Steen. Silently asking, "Why is Baratium here?"

"Walter, get these... filthy mongrels dressed. I have no desire to see proof of their existence, much less their phallically grotesque forms," demands his master. "I intend to move them today."

Shocked faces search other shocked faces throughout the room. Many stare open-mouthed. Kick watches Walter who has a maniacal sneer creep across his face. While the shock of Baratium's statement settles in, Bladriell conjures black robes and belts out of thin air. He passes them to the prisoners who whisper to each other.

After they're dressed Baratium speaks again. "Walter, separate the gargoyle filth from the others. Then you need to take those others to your laboratory." Baratium laughs then leaves his minion to work. Walter separates them as ordered. He kicks and pushes, shoving his was through them, making little headway, so he resorts to insults then starts ramming a magical staff into them like a cattle prod. The sneer he is wearing is mixed with glee at whatever they have planned for the goyles. He and Bladriell force several of the gargoyles to his laboratory not sparing the prod. They make them wait before a jump buoy. That's a stone that makes it possible to move several people and/or things simultaneously to another place. The buoys can also anchor a soul, so they don't get lost and can be recalled.

Kick notices that Walter is moving the captives in small groups. Worried about another attempt on his pathetic life.

As the cages empty and the room clears, Kick asks, "Where's everyone going?"

"The master is sending them to different places to serve his purposes," Walter retorts.

Kick didn't want to press his luck, so he lets it drop. Kick, Peter, and Steen are all who remain in the final cage.

When they're moved to Walter's laboratory, he orders, "Stand there, next to the jump buoy with the others." Walter points at the large shaped rock in the center of his lab.

Kick recognizes this jump buoy as the Ceorfan queen's. How the cruel Walter came to possess it is beyond comprehension. *This is a terrible sign. Have the Ceorfan survived the war?* Since their imprisonment, this is the first time he considers giving up all hope of escape or returning home.

"Walter, what happened to Kino and the other gargoyles? Did you send them somewhere?" Kick asks.

Walter turns and considers Kick for a second. "Under what circumstances do you foresee me answering your questions?" he says sneering.

Loathsome Walter jumps Kick, Peter, Steen and a few other mages to what can only be described as a stone fortress. Unlike the portal stone where they would walk through one at a time as if down a tunnel. The jump buoy is different, one second, they're in Walter's laboratory and the next they're inside a stone citadel. The mages look around hoping for an escape route. Not finding a visible one Kick states, "Unquestionably, we're in the Fae realm."

"Very astute, Kick. You and the others shall also have full freedom to walk about the fortress, its grounds and surrounding areas, with a few limitations. All provided you never attempt to leave," Walter says.

The three Ceorfan mages turn unsure how to respond. They see Walter Deveros standing there with a triumphant smile, his hands tucked inside his robes. Kick and the others know well how fast he is with spells, so they don't bother trying to rush him.

"Since my master has given me permission, I'm excited to tell you you'll no longer assist him to build his Crafted army. It's now large enough."

With that, Kick stands straight as an arrow, a genuine smile creeping over the corners of his mouth. He places a hand on the shoulder of his friends Peter and Steen. They pat each other on the back congratulating one another for surviving the ordeal. Kick can't believe his good luck. That's the thing about Walter nothing good is ever free. Although his last question was refused, Kick ever unfazed by setbacks asks, "Why do we get to stop torturing our friends, Walter?"

"Well, that's because Baratium Mezacain has rid his realm of the filthy gargoyles. He destroyed your friend Kino last, I believe. My master said he wanted Kino to see his friends destroyed before his own destruction. A fitting end," Walter gloats.

The joy that had wrapped its arms around them, now squeezes them so hard Kick can't breathe. He drops to his knees and screams. His cry as much anger as pain and stares at Walter, his reprehensible visage burned into Kick's memory. *There'll come a day Walter when I'll destroy you. I'll burn you piece by piece until only your head and heart remain. And those I'll fill with the pain of each one of my friends that you have destroyed.*

With that final abuse, Walter spins on a heel and leaves almost skipping.

The prisoners stand in shock. Kick sits on his heels his toes carrying his weight, his arms hanging at his sides. For each of them, the pain is as real as if it happened in front of them. The deaths of these gargoyles represent more than the end of a dear friend. These gargoyles were family.

12

THE FUCKWIT

KICK IS THE FIRST TO MOVE. HE STANDS. NOT BY LEANING forward and pushing up with his hands. Not even by pulling himself up using the window ledge as a hold. He leans back onto the flat of his feet into a squat, then up. Kick wants to show the others he hasn't given up and neither should they. "If I said we will destroy this mother-fucker, who's with me?" Kick asks in a soft voice.

The other three men in the room turn his direction. All three of them grab his arm in a salute of shared obligation. Together they stand with Kick in their mutual 'kill or be killed' opposition to Baratium and Walter.

"Make no mistake, this'll not be easy or quick. But to do this, we need to gather information. Walter said we're in the Fae realm. I only believe him because my magic seems stronger." There was a general buzz of agreement.

"He also said he's giving us the freedom to roam as long as we don't leave," Peter adds. "I'll bet if we leave they'll kill our families."

"So, we've got the run of this place, 'within reason,' whatever the fuck that means. If we take a chance and it doesn't pan out, someone we love will die. We also need to steal the staff from that fucker Baratium and plan our escape. Is this about right?" Steen asks.

"That's right... so any ideas on why the three of them move around inside this realm so easily? My guess is their blood's got enough Fae blood in it, they're recognized as Fae," Peter asserts.

Steen answers, "I agree."

Kick's been listening to his two friends while thinking through what has happened today. "I'd agree with you both, but I'd also go further and bet that fuckhead Baratium must be fae. That's how he's got this fortress. It must be his residence. You can't live here unless you're fae. This and his ability to travel freely, including bringing in slaves like us is a dead giveaway." The others nod in agreement waiting on Kick to continue. "I'm also betting the fae don't like us much because we're Ceorfan and help humans. And since the fuckwit Baratium brought us here as slaves, the fae would enslave us, or they could use us for their own entertainment."

"Entertainment?" Steen queries.

"Yeah, the fae, depending on their mood, think killing humans, even humans who can make spells is entertainment. Unless there's something in it for them, they will do the same thing to you. I might be exempt being half fae," Kick answers.

Bladriell returns and directs Kick and the others to their rooms. They're each given a private one. Although it doesn't contain much beyond a bed, it is still a room.

THE MONOTONY of their day runs one day into the next. Their captors teach them a new spell and make them practice it, it's for a fight. They tell the Ceorfan mages this spell will kill.

Kick has learned a handful of spells now. The days muddied his sense of time. *A month has passed... longer, who knows... who cares?* His friends are dead. Today Bladriell and Walter come to talk to all three mages in Kick's room. They inform them they will attack and destroy a small clan of fae. The asshat apprentice hands them a map of the area. The ass says, "The mission is for the current king of the fae. There are seven or eight of these fae who you will kill. The unlucky bastards challenged the right of the king to rule. You'll find them at the location I've marked upon your map. You three will have the advantage of the spells I've taught you and the element of surprise."

"Why should we care about protecting this... king? Can't he fight his own battles?" Kick retorts.

"Yeah, if he's a king..." Peter starts before he's cut off by Bladriell motioning with a finger slice across his neck.

Walter pipes up, "You agreed, whether you like it or not, you would support our master Baratium Mezacain. In return for your fealty, he agreed to keep your friends and family safe. He's doing his part. It will be a shame if you force him to reconsider his position. However, you're correct, it's your choice." He talks loudly, adds a grin, and makes it clear they are putting their loved ones in jeopardy if they refuse.

"So, what shall it be, will you do as you promised or not?" Walter croaks.

Disgusted by the 'do as I say, or your family dies' retort from their captor, they agree.

"Good," Bladriell takes over, "you'll leave in the morning. Go to bed, it'll be an early day for you tomorrow." He and the rusty-haired shit leave together.

WHILE THEY SLEEP Baratium injects visions into Kick's dreams. They are nightmare visions of what Baratium will do to Kick's parents if he questions another order again. The nightmares are vivid. Kick is sure he saw what happened and not just a night terror.

The horror doesn't end in the death of either of his parents. Yet the torture involved makes certain Kick will never question an order again. If he could just see his mom.

The look on Peter and Steen's faces the next morning tell Kick he knows they have had the same experiences. They won't speak of it. Their incubus is named Baratium Mezacain, and they now choose to obey his every command.

Walter jumps them to their location. They destroy the clan and return.

Upon their return, they return to their training routine. Learn... practice... fight... kill... This routine becomes their life. Time no longer has any meaning. It has even less meaning when Kick remembers time inside the Fae realm runs differently than outside Fae. He may leave to act as an assassin for Baratium, enter the human realm, then return to Fae. He may return years later even though it has been mere hours for him.

Kick has murdered so often, in the name of protecting his family, he decides nothing matters to him anymore, least of all his life. For Kick, there's no way to escape this personal hell, he's become an abomination to himself. Left with only one way to control his fate, he decides to starve himself. *The food is terrible anyway...* even this small inside joke offers no respite for Kick. His life is useless. It's better to die. He hides that he isn't eating by feeding his rations to the rats infesting the garrison they inhabit. He drinks water, believing the lack of water would be too obvious and they will discover what he's doing before he's ready. The meager rations he's given, do little to ensure his health. The decline to death is short.

After less than a week Kick is confident he can finish his starvation. During the week, he loses his desire to even sip his water. Fatigue is part of his life and now becomes overwhelming as his fast continues. On what he believes is his final day, his weakness is profound, and he can't get out of his bed to retrieve the water left by his door. *The absence of food and now water... this will end faster.*

Kick's thoughts go to Drusey. To that day at the beach. The meal they shared. Her wicked little smile before they made love. Kick falls into the memory reaching for every breath and nuance reliving it as if it just happened. Kick laughs softly as he closes his eyes knowing he has no intention of ever opening them again.

13

THE LONG SLEEP

THAT EVENING, CREEPY BLADRIELL IS SPEAKING WITH WALTER in his office area of the fortress laboratory. They are resting, talking, and drinking coffee. On a table in the lab's middle sit two sealed opaque jars with a short length of twine secured to the top. Bewildered by what he sees, Bladriell asks his fellow fiend, "What's this?"

Walter, trying to build a stronger rapport with his pupil, declares, "This my friend is our entertainment. Bladriell, ever pulled the wings off of flies?" At this, Walter removes the opacity from the containers, revealing that there are faeries in each jar. The creepy apprentice's eyes grow wide with anticipation. For the next several hours, the two cretins entertain themselves through various means of persecution of the small individuals. The final torture is placing the beings back into the jars and spinning them in circles using the attached string. The winner is the one whose faery can make it through a maze before they die. Neither of the poor creatures survive. Happy with the day's entertainment the two vile flunkies get to work. They leave their conversation off and immersed themselves in activity. Walter writing and re-writing spells for experiments and Bladriell cleaning and organizing.

With squinting eyes, Walter his parchment and quill in hand stops like he has just remembered something and asks, "Apprentice, deliver me one of the Ceorfan mages. I have a murder I need committed, and I require one of them to get it done."

"Walter, you realize there are only three of them? He thinks that he will have to do the killings if they are all killed in the dangerous situations Walter keeps sending them into.

"I need the killing completed," Walter says. He proceeds to scrape the pen across his page immersed in his study.

"Yes, Walter."

"Good, very good. However, we should safeguard them if we have so few left, there is more we need before their demise. We need them to assist us as of now. So, bring me a mage." He drifts back to his task.

"Do you care which one?" Bladriell persists.

"They're equally talented, why would I care?" The grizzled old shit is becoming irritated at having to divide his attention and levels a sinister look at the assistant.

"Okay, I'll get Steen," Bladriell said, not caring for the manner his teacher is treating him.

Bladriell leaves the cluttered room and returns with Steen. The ancient mage doesn't look up or acknowledge those entering the chamber.

"Walter, here's Steen," the apprentice prods. His teacher doesn't glance at Steen. Instead, he looks through Bladriell to someplace in the past. "Apprentice I've changed my mind. I want the mage, Gortanik instead."

"May I ask why?" Bladriell asks exasperatedly.

"I don't remember seeing him in the last day. I think I should see him. Bladriell take this one back. I'll use Gortanik for this deed."

"Steen, return to your room," Bladriell barks.

Steen shrugs his shoulders turns and leaves. The agitated young pupil heads down a nearby corridor to Kick's room and opens his door.

The room's dark. There are no candles lit. He digs into his robe and fishing out his wand Bladriell ignites one with a wave. In the flickering light, he discovers Kick lying on his back in bed. His eyes are closed. "Gortanik, what are you dreaming about?" Bladriell demands.

Kick, doesn't move a muscle.

"Damn it, man, that must be some wet dream. Wake up now!" This time he shakes Kick hard, his frustration mounting. It's here that Kick's face takes shape. His sunken eyes... the blackness surrounding them... his lips are cracked. Bladriell recognizes that Kick is starving himself. He checks for a pulse. Creepy Bladriell detects a faint, rapid heartbeat. He spells the sick Ceorfan into a druid sleep then rushes to tell that shithead Walter what's happening. Walter is still sitting in his lab. Lazy bastard never moves unless he's forced. He's not writing but reading.

Bladriell comes into the chamber and watches his employer. He guesses they received a new a set of orders from Baratium. The master sends his acolyte orders via an enchanted parchment. A duplicate to a scroll Walter keeps in his possession one that mirrors Baratium's. Their new orders are clear, Walter is to transcribe the orders onto a blank parchment and destroy the enchanted one. The eradication, according to Baratium, will also destroy the magical scroll in Baratium's possession. It stuns Walter as he completes the transcription and elimination of both charmed manuscripts. He needs this completed because the parchments contain magic that will give away their plans to Baratium's captors.

The angry young apprentice waits for Walter's instructions. He's concerned given the old mage's concentration. Then his boss jerks to his feet, the look on his face scaring Bladriell.

Walter shouts, "They captured him! They did it. They captured him and are about to encase him in a glass prison! The enemy captured him and is placing him inside a prison bottle." He is making no sense.

"Walter, who is captured?" Bladriell asks.

"Baratium Mezacain," Walter spits.

Hearing those words, the creepy little Bladriell freezes in place. Walter's evil, but he isn't stupid. He knows his apprentice follows their master for gold. The very funds he sees evaporating before his mind's eye. He also knows the king of this realm will be no help, he has no love for Baratium. He has a great desire to receive the large bribes.

Okay, so Walter has Mezacain's orders. They need to find and release their master. Creepy Bladriell is slow but piecing the information together.

Walter's slimy voice utters, "I have a plan to rescue him and make a fortune in gold at the same time. And the Ceorfan scum will help us." At this, they both laugh. Well, Walter laughs while Bladriell screeches. They imagine life with the loss of wealth and joyous at their plan to save it.

Bladriell stops screeching, remembering he needs to inform his leader about Kick. He says, "I found Gortanik almost dead. He's been starving himself, and he almost succeeded. I put him in a druid sleep."

"Good, good job, Bladriell! Keep him in the druid sleep. He'll be forced to heal. Who are the other mages still alive?"

"Along with Gortanik, we have Peter and Steen."

"Okay, Bladriell, the Ceorfan mages don't know Baratium's a prisoner. They also know nothing about the prison bottle he's now sure to be hidden inside. We mention nothing about Baratium's capture and tell the Fae nothing. We'll put the other two mages in a druid sleep too. After they are in their sleep, we'll prepare our fortress to protect us while we wait."

"Wait for what?" Bladriell asks slow on the uptake.

"Our master to return. After we've prepared, we'll also begin the druid sleep. However, we will wake at the mention of Baratium's name." Together they laugh their scheming laugh again. At this, Walter is sure he has Bladriell on his team.

The two fiends put Peter and Steen into a deep druid sleep

beside Kick. Then, like little ants, they set to work. Walter sets Crafted throughout the fortress to act as protectors. He sets some to work on the outside of the stronghold making sure nothing can come within a kilometer of their walls. For his last task, he places another group of servants he's hired from Fae to work as tenders, both to the bodies which lie in druid sleep, but their fortress as well. These fae will ensure the sleeping bodies are bathed and covered as needed for whatever weather conditions. They'll also ensure their citadel is maintained.

While Walter is setting the fae to work, the slimy Bladriell busies himself with spells. He sets a recall for Walter for any time that the name Baratium is mentioned. It's a simple spell which activates if a person says the name of Baratium, or finds the bottle. When activated, Walter's druid sleep will be broken first, then Bladriell's. He then sets other spells to seal the entrances of the garrison and every door and passageway throughout the structure. The only thing able to enter or leave is the Crafted and fae servants. Finally, he sets an alarm for himself should shithead Walter try to leave him.

After they set everything, the two henchmen go their separate ways to their rooms and begin their druid sleep.

Hundreds of years pass. Walter awakens several times to find himself disappointed. He finds no clues to the location of the bottle or their master. Each time, he reenters the druid sleep. This sleep, wake, sleep cycle continues for hundreds of years. Then one day...

14

AWAKE

Walter is wakened from his healing sleep by the alarm... someone said Baratium's name. He decides, after investigation, this is a clue that will net him his master's prison bottle. They have found it. It's been generations of false leads, but this time there's a strong possibility of success. He is meeting a traitor to the Ceorfan Guild in an underground facility he's spelled to appear as a thriving place of work for a rebellion against the humans. The traitor's name is Traver. The typical gargoyle has only one name, but this ass calls himself 'Council Member Traver.' The grizzled old mage knows the traitor agrees with him on killing the human infestation. He also knows that the traitor doesn't have a clue the bottle is his master's prison. It says Baratium on the glass, so he understands it is most likely his. He thinks its only value is magical and doesn't know Walter wants to use the goyles as servants for his cause. He'll keep that secret for now.

THE CONNIVING MAGE is at the underground meeting place when a skinny gargoyle arrives. He's here to meet with Walter, who's in league with the banished Baratium. Traver has the bottle which holds the exiled mage, hidden in his cloak. He's been negotiating with the ancient mage over the rights to the bottle. Traver has never been interested in selling the item until recently. Now there's a new Ceorfan queen, and Traver senses his power slipping so things have changed. Traver's always had power within the Guild offering advice to the rulers. The skinny traitor used his position to steal Baratium's bottle and replace it with a fake. He's going to use it and another item he's 'gained' to regain his power and multiply his wealth far beyond any other gargoyle.

Walking up to the traitor Walter asks, "Have you brought the bottle for me?"

"What, no hello, Walter? Fine then. Have you brought my gold?"

"Yes. So, give me the bottle, and we can be finished."

"Wait a moment Walter, I am not finished with you. I've another treasure I wish you to see first." The High Guild Member Traver removes a crystal headed staff, the Caor Thintri, which was Baratium's staff. "So, you see Walter, I believe you may want to purchase this other item too."

Walter looks at the staff, then back at Traver. "How much for the staff?"

"I am not greedy. I only want two small things. Double the amount of gold and jewels and a place in Baratium's council."

Walter's at a loss. He looks at Bladriell for an answer written on his face. Finding nothing, he turns to Traver and responds, "I only brought the treasure for the bottle for now. I'll get it for the staff if you swear fealty to my master Baratium."

Traver's chest expands gloating and anticipating that he'll soon command the power he craves and knowing he has the ancient mage where he wants him. "Walter, I'll only sell this as a package deal. You must purchase them both, or receive neither. Send another bat with a message when you are ready to meet. I'll meet you here on the full moon after receiving the message."

"Agreed," Walter says. Now that the discussion is over Traver turns and leaves. Bladriell comes out of his hiding place and strolls over to his teacher.

"So, where do we go from here, Walter?"

"My friend, this will be like taking candy from a baby. We'll wake the Ceorfan mages and force them to steal the treasure we need. To do that, we will trick them into being your ally. There's no way one of them will ever trust me," schemes Walter.

"That'll be my job. I can do that," the creepy pupil says.

They eat, drink, and discuss their plan for tricking the Ceorfan mages into believing to gain their freedom they must free another mage who promises to save them from Walter and Baratium. To release the mage, they'll lie to the Ceorfan. And tell them they need to steal gold and jewels to purchase what we need to survive or something similar. Hopefully by the time they have enough funds for the traitor, Bladriell will have them befriended and believing in his cause to release the mage in the bottle. "Even after they've stolen enough wealth, we'll have them continue to steal so they'll feel they're fulfilling a purpose," Walter adds, "the key to this whole project is you must convince them you are on their side."

"I can convince them of that. Have you got any ideas on how to persuade them?" Bladriell asks.

"You'll convince them you have been tortured just as they were, and you had to do as Baratium and I requested to keep your family safe! After we have collected enough treasure, I'll retrieve the staff and bottle. Then we can have them assist us, of their own free wills, with freeing our master," Walter declares. The whole plan is materializing in his head. The rusty-haired old mage makes sure that his protégé understands the key is to make friends with Kick. He must believe the creepy liar is telling the truth about being just as tortured as the Ceorfan. Walter instructs Bladriell how the world has changed since they entered the druid sleep. But it's now easier to find treasure than it was before. "In the African hills, there is a place where they mine diamonds. Diamonds are worth quite a lot in this time period.

That is where we'll begin. Our first step is to wake the Ceorfan mages."

AWAKE and physically healthy each of the Ceorfan warrior mages drink deeply from a cup that Bladriell hands them. It's drugged but Kick is so thirsty he might drink piss right now.

"What are you drugging me with, Bladriell?" Kick asks the mage who has remained in the background since their capture.

"It is opium from the orient. I'm sorry, Gortanik but maybe it'll help to dull the pain. I use it for that when I'm not able to cope sometimes," answers the assistant mage. Bladriell had earlier cast a spell on himself making his voice deeper and carry a charm which will make others more susceptible to his suggestions.

His voice is lovely, a deep tone full of care. This is one of the few times Kick has spoken with Bladriell. Kick looks the apprentice up and down wondering if it is the opium or if he's misjudged the young assistant.

The lying schemer confides that he's also a prisoner of Baratium, just as they are. "I am one of the Hewn. The Hewn are wandering nomads of the Ceorfan Guild. Many of my brethren have also been imprisoned by Baratium to be carved. Walter and Baratium lied to you about your friends. They are all alive and free. Your queen freed them, but they hid you away, so the Ceorfan queen never knew you were here. They let your friends go because they had taken mine. My family remains safe because I do as I'm told. My younger sister lives in a nomadic tribe close to the Aegean Sea, near where they captured you. I want her to remain free and safe."

"Then, you understand our pain, and know we want to escape?" Kick asks.

"I do. I would help you if I could. The only thing I can possibly do to help you is to give you something to dull the pain," Bladriell says as Kick drifts into a haze of euphoria.

Kick relives the time he spent with his family and Drusey. It isn't real, on some level he knows this, but it's a better place than where he is now. He plans to get up soon and check on his brothers... when he isn't so high.

The other mages receive the same treatment from Bladriell. But at the end of every conversation, they don't care about much, as they sink deep into the drug haze.

15

ADDICTED

AFTER WEEKS OF BEING SUPPLIED WITH DRUGS, THE THREE Ceorfan warrior mages are thoroughly devoted to opium. Kick lies in his bed in the garrison in Fae. The exhilaration of the opium high gone. The muscle aches, tremors, and nausea have yet to begin. His headache is starting to burn through his mind. It's only beginning, but Kick can tell from experience this one will be massive.

He desires more of the drug and Bladriell is late with his dose. Kick decides to get up and find the errant colleague. On his way, he pays no attention to the fresh air or the sunshine. Kick's on a mission, and nothing else matters. He meets Peter and stops dead in his tracks. At least the caricature of the man he had known is standing in front of him. The imitation man shocks Kick enough that his mission loses its purpose. Peter's wasting may be the only thing which could have deterred him from completing it, anyway.

Kick stands, palms at his sides. Peter's once muscle-bound body is now shrunken. His skin clings to him in a semblance of pleated curtains where it once was taut. His definition hasn't entirely faded, but now absent are his bulk along with the animalistic power he once possessed. Kick feels an overwhelming need to help him, followed immediately by a sudden flash of their friendship and of how he has failed them all. Peter and Steen had been his friends. Guilt slams him. He should have found them a way out of this place long ago.

"Peter, I've missed you so much," he says. The dark Ceorfan grabs his old friend and hugs him gently, afraid to break him. Reality sinks in that he's also an addict and hasn't cared about his life either.

"Kick, is that you? You look strange? I'm hooked on opium, are you too?" he asks.

"Yes, and it has helped me, but it's time for me to start to live and fight. I've forgotten to fight. Peter do you have it in you to help. I won't blame you if you can't."

"I'm not sure I can, but I'll try. Do you know where the others are?"

"Let's make that our first mission," Kick suggests.

Both have a renewed mission and start to look for their friends. They find Steen, but he's the only one they find. Oh yeah, everyone else is dead, right? They're out of energy. Together they make a pact to help one another but still need the drug. So, they'll take it, but try to wean themselves off given the chance. They are tired and fall asleep in Steen's room.

That's how Bladriell finds them. He wakes them one at a time and has them carefully drink the opium he's prepared. "Please don't waste any of it. Now that you're able to get around some on your own, I need to have your help."

"What kind of help?" Kick asks.

"Guys, what you have got to understand is, things are extremely different in this day and age. You do remember, we were forced to sleep in the druid sleep for many centuries. Drugs aren't easy to buy any more," Bladriell lies.

"Again, I ask, what kind of help?" Kick asks more forcefully.

"Okay, I need you to steal some jewels. Steal us some treasure so that I can afford to buy more of the opium for us."

Peter, Steen, and Kick stare at each other, each waiting for another to speak first. Finally Kick answers, "Yeah. No trouble. Remember Bladriell we won't hurt anybody for you though."

"Good. I don't want anyone hurt either. I'm trying to help us right now."

"Okay, what do we need to do?" Steen asks.

"There's a small village in Africa. They have loads of diamonds. They practically find them on the ground there. You'll take some Crafted, raid the village and take all the diamonds you can find. I will spell them to obey you for the time. Don't worry about the villagers they will have the jewels replaced in a few weeks, so you're really not doing anything but causing them some minor inconvenience," Bladriell explains.

His explanation convinces the Ceorfan mages. After more planning and preparation, the three are ready to leave. "Okay Bladriell, we're ready," Peter tells him as the three walk toward him. Peter's in the middle, flanked by Steen and Kick. Suddenly Kick stumbles, and Bladriell has to help catch him.

"Sorry man. The drugs make me stumble sometimes," Kick apologizes. Bladriell laughs.

He's still working on making them like and trust him. "No problem. We help each other, right?"

None of the three answers, but Kick pats Bladriell on the shoulder.

The mages leave, taking their Crafted monsters with them. When they arrive in the South African village, they round up all the humans in the town and assign the Crafted guard to watch them.

Kick can find things he needs. His talent works for him as he uses his magic to his advantage. He casts the spell and concentrates on what he wants to find. In this case, the jewels. Even as high on the opium as they are, complete with their faltering and silly laughing, they find a lot of pillage.

Now, that he is away from the fortress Kick has a spark of hope. It might be possible to escape. Well, being away from the garrison, combined with his earlier theft from Bladriell! The three of them had planned to steal a portal stone from Bladriell. Their walking directly at him and Kick 'accidentally' stumbling into him was a ruse for the dark-haired warrior to pickpocket the stone. He is a practiced cutpurse and had used his talent several times to the chagrin of his parents. His coup was a perfect success. Kick knocking into Bladriell was just the bonus!

As they collect jewels and return to the residents one of them begins to argue with the mages. "Sicela musa ukweba amadayimane yami! Sicela musa ukweba amadayimane yami!" He yells pointing at the bag containing their loot.

Kick smiles. He speaks many languages and understands the man enough even though there are differences since he had learned the language.

"Kuthiwani ngezohweboso?" Kick replies.

The man stops, looking somewhat confused that this white man can speak their language. After pausing briefly, he pushes his son toward Kick and says, "Msize yena nami ngizokunika okufunayo."

Kick smiles... again.

Peter asks, "What are you two going on about?"

"Well, this good man is the leader in this Zulu village, and he doesn't want us to steal his diamonds. I asked him if I could trade him something. He said if I could help his son he'd trade. I know I can help the boy. He's starving and just needs to have a good diet." Kick lifts the boy onto his lap and asks him if he is hungry. The little one stares at him, and with tears running down his little cheeks, he nods his head, "Yes."

Kick says, "I know what to do. You guys keep an eye on these monsters and make sure they don't hurt the villagers. I'll be right back. If Bladriell shows up, cover for me."

Kick pulls the recently stolen portal stone from his tattered robe and opens a portal. Kick's trying to go to where he thinks he'll find a farmer to get the child some milk. Or better yet, the cow! When the portal closes behind Kick, he realizes he is in a thriving metropolis and is standing beside a huge indoor market full of food. *This can't be right, I'm in the wrong country. Well, that's what traveling high does for you, dumbass.*

He isn't dressed to blend in at all. So, with a wave of his hand, he's wearing black slacks like the gentleman who just passed by him and a black hoodie like another. Now, he's generally being ignored, so he strides into the store. He notices a young redheaded woman carrying a small child with curly blond hair but who is still very much like the one from the village.

He asks her, "Excuse me, what do you feed your child?"

She looks at him, sizing him up. With a genuine smile, she replies, "Oh Lord help me! You must be another new father! I declare. If you ain't the third man, I've had to help this week. They sure do need to start teaching this stuff in our Texas schools! Ok, darlin', so your wife sent you to the store to buy formula. Grab a cart and follow me." Then without another word, she heads further into the market.

Kick quickly takes ahold of a cart like hers and rushes to catch her. The front two wheels are squeaking loudly and are shaking so badly, that controlling the cart is difficult.

After he catches up to his helper, she proceeds to teach him all about the formula. Kick can speak many languages, including English. But getting used to her use of the language takes him a few seconds. After her explanation, he fills the entire basket with the cans the lady shows him. He asks her, "Is there really milk for a child in this container?"

She smiles at him, and while patting him on the hand, she says, "Trust me, honey. Are you sure you're gonna need that much? Oh, dear Lord, help me you must have triplets! My, oh my."

Wait, 'honey.' I thought it was milk?

She just shrugs her shoulders, turns, and leaves. Kick chooses to say nothing else as he follows her to the checkout line. He watches the others in the surrounding lines. They all seem to have this plastic card that they use to pay for their groceries. So, he makes one magically, which looks like theirs, but when he plugs it into the scanner, it doesn't work. He spells the cashier into believing he's paid. She pushes a few buttons, tells him, "Thank you." Then she hands him a long piece of paper with numbers on it. He stuffs it into his pocket and walks to a secluded area and portals back to the village with his prize, cart and all.

He smiles when he sees the malnourished little boy. He quickly opens one of the containers and has the boys drink some milk or honey formula. Then he pulls the cart filled with the other cans of the milk-honey to the boy's father. The man is so happy with the exchange that he gives Kick more diamonds than he hoped they would find.

Before they leave, Kick takes the paper receipt out of his pocket and gives it to the man. If Walter and Bladriell, find it, they will know he had left, and he would certainly be punished. They may even take his parents' lives.

Peter and Steen also search for any drugs they can pocket, so they don't have to depend on Bladriell as much. After their search, they do find drugs, they take their haul and head back to the fortress.

Upon arrival, they don't find Bladriell. Well at least, not right away. Soon though, he walks into Kick's room where the three mages are waiting for him. He seems a little happier than usual, but Kick decides not to comment. Bladriell, however, does take notice of Kick's new clothes and asks, "Where did you get the clothes, Gortanik?"

"I saw them in the village and took them. What do you think? They're better than the stuff you give us," Kick answers.

The evil assistant shakes his head judging Kick's new clothes. "I have an idea that I can find some better stuff. I'll get to work on it. Keep them if you like. Just don't let Walter see you in them. He doesn't know you're helping me get the gold or jewels to buy the opium. I plan on telling him. I just haven't done it yet." Bladriell is plainly still trying to fool the prisoners into trusting him. He believes they're coming along, but he's also sure they're still wary of him. He also knows they're still plotting ways of escape from their prison... without anyone, they love ending up dead.

16

PLANS AND TRAITORS

On a trip to inform Walter how the mission went Bladriell smiles to himself, happy he believes he is fooling his 'new found friends.' Included in his report will be that the Crafted destroyed the entire South African village after Kick, Peter, and Steen left, just as he and Walter had planned.

The laboratory has a strange feel tonight as he enters and wonders what is that horrid smell? He holds his breath for a second waiting for his teacher to acknowledge him.

When the grizzled old ass glances up, he rolls his eyes. He asks, "You have something to share?"

"Yes, Commander, I need to give you my report." He continues after seeing his master nod. "Gortanik doesn't know that I've got a tracking spell on him. I let him think he stole a portal stone from me. He used it to open a portal to a market in America where he bought food for the villagers as a trade for diamonds. The minute Gortanik spoke the spell tipped me off of his whereabouts. I'm trying to win his confidence, so I didn't let him know, but Walter, we've got to get a tighter control on that mage," Bladriell explains.

Walter agrees, "I think you're right and I have just the person. Do you remember my sister Trix? She can control anyone by addicting them to sex. Up the opium doses and I'll get them each a satyriatrix, of their own."

"I haven't ever heard of that. What is it? Is your sister named after the type of faery she is?" Bladriell asks.

"Yes, and like I said Bladriell, she can addict people to sex. Once addicted to her, she's able to use sex as a wedge against them by guilting them into doing as she says. Combining this sex addiction with the opium addiction should make them less observant and more compliant. Trix and her friends are a little like the sirens. Only my sister uses sex instead of a song. I'll see my sister and make an offer. I'll pay her and her friends in diamonds for their services. Afterward, I must jump to meet that gargoyle, Traver, now that we have the full amount for the Coar Thintri and the bottle prison our master is inside. I'll see you in the morning. Don't forget Bladriell, ensure you give the Ceorfan mages extra opium," Walter orders.

Turning away, Walter uses the jump buoy in his laboratory to journey to his sister's home. She lives a few miles off the shore of the mainland Fae realm. Trix is a dark beauty with rainbow colored hair. She's everything one can imagine in a desirable partner. After hugs and a short visit Walter starts, "I need your help to control some prisoners. We need their help with waking Baratium, and the only way they will help is through trickery. I'm getting his prison bottle from a Ceorfan dissident. As soon as I retrieve it, I'll need these mages to help free Baratium. Afterward, we'll begin the process of ridding the world of the human pestilence. We are nearing the time when we will rise to dominance over the humans."

Walter pictures himself as a great orator; this is his most recent affirmation. On some level, he believes what he is saying. The question is, does he consider himself capable of carrying out the steps necessary to bring about the freedom of his master?

Baratium, has promised those who assist him land, slaves, and even magic tools. So, Walter promises Trix an island and a priceless crown which makes the wearer young and beautiful for life. At this moment he must bribe her to get her to provide the help he needs. For now, Walter is ready with a substantial purse filled with diamonds, jewels, and rare stones. One stone is about the size of a large gold coin, it glows a light-blue.

He warns, "Trix, it's important that you ensure that this mage, Gortanik, is under your spell. I need you to find two of your trusted friends to do the same to the other two mages, his friends Peter and Steen. I need all three Ceorfan mages to help me free Baratium. Together, Bladriell and I do not have enough power to break that spell without the help of dragon blood. The supply of dragon blood we had gained was wasted long ago, so we must compensate with more magic. Use these to pay your other friends. The glowing light-blue one, we took from the last Ceorfan dragon queen. Keep that one away from these mages."

"Don't worry brother, I'm looking forward to this," Trix replies, "now scoot so I can get ready. I want to find the best helpers for the other mages. We'll be there tonight. It's best to start when they're asleep. They sleep at night, don't they?"

"They sleep most of the time now because they're drugged. Trix, thank you for your help. Here's a portal stone to take you and your friends to the fortress. I'll see you there tonight. For now, I need to leave. I'm late for an appointment." With that, Walter jumps again. This time to the coast of the Black Sea, near a tavern in a rundown Hewn village.

This is the same Hewn tavern as the one where he and Traver met for the first time. The bar is large and not as well-lit as Walter prefers. What do you expect from rodents who live in bat shit? The tavern is empty this time of the night. Most of the Hewn have work. The few who are here are travelers. Hewn, who don't even stay within a group of their own kind.

In the dusky light, Walter spots the Ceorfan High Guild Member. The High Guild is a much-esteemed position because they provide advice to the queen. The new Ceorfan queen, the old mage believes, will begin her reign by respecting tradition and including following the advice of those who sit on the High Guild. Walter spies the staff that the arrogant skinny gargoyle has hidden under his coat and decides if he has to kill Traver he will have the staff and prison bottle tonight.

The rusty old mage keeps his greedy eyes on Traver, not wanting to show even a hint of excitement. He asks with a serious tone, "Have you brought the bottle and staff?"

"You have seen the staff, I have the prison bottle hidden nearby. Do you have the payment?" Traver returns.

Taking out a small chest full of diamonds Walter tells him, "This is more than what I promised, so I want both items now."

Traver pauses, staring into Walter's eyes. "Before I bring you the bottle, I want assurances that my position in the new order under Baratium, will allow for myself and my men positions above all others," Traver demands.

"How many men are we talking?"

"Five including myself."

"Then we have a deal. I'll be sure to guarantee your positions when our master takes over this plane," alleges Walter. He's lying through his teeth, and if Bladriell were here, he would have had him freeze and kill the man just to have him out of the way. That gives him an idea. He's going to trick the traitor with a fake image of his master. It will be an easy trick, but should instill enough fear to control him.

Again, Traver pauses. Then deciding, he glances across the room at another gargoyle who had been sitting alone in the corner, who stands and walks to them. He hands Traver an item wrapped in thick padding. Traver hands it over to Walter who puts it in one of the many pockets of his mage robe. Then he reaches for the staff. The mage stops him and says, "My Master wants you to give this straight to him. He is waiting behind the building. Come with me. Don't speak to him or he will kill you. Hand him the item and leave immediately. I will give you your reward inside." They walk into the dark alley. When Traver sees what he thinks is Baratium, his breathing stops, and his body shakes, but he completes his task as commanded and leaves. He doesn't wait for his partner in crime, he is scared. Inside the Hewn establishment, he waits with a face washed out of all color. Spying Walter beside him, he puts out his hands for the chest of diamonds that is his pay. The rusty haired old mage hands it to him and commands, "If you need anything else use a portal stone and leave a message in locker 155 at the bus station in Prague. Oh, and Traver, keep TASS off our asses."

Walter turns to leave, giddy with the excitement of retrieving the prison bottle and the staff. He jumps back to the stone fortress of Baratium in Faery. Neither the gargoyles nor the humans know the remnants of Baratium's army have been hiding in the Fae realm. Walter hadn't even told the traitor Traver even though he thinks Traver may become a trusted ally.

Walter's so excited at pulling off the recovery of both prizes he's buzzing with it when he returns to his laboratory. He is talking to the bottle prison as he locks it up in a safe and puts a magical alarm on it for safety. He speaks to the bottle, "In just a few more days master we will have you out of your prison."

That's when Bladriell enters the lab and puts his stash of opium away. He reports to Walter that the three Ceorfan mages are all lost in their drug-hazed minds. They laugh and leave to have dinner together and discuss more of their plans to free their master.

17

COMPANY IN THE NIGHT

DEEP IN THE GARRISON KICK IS LEANING BACK ON HIS BED enjoying his opium-induced euphoria. He is dozing when he prepares to dream of Drusey. The memory hits him like a hurricane, but he still enjoys dreaming of her, even if it tears his heart out when he remembers she's gone. He thinks of her as much as his mind will let him. The rest of his dreams are nightmares. Tonight, however, is excellent.

In this dream, he sees a woman who he is sure isn't Drusey, but he likes her all the same. Her beauty is undeniable and overpowering. When his fantasy girl comes to him and touches his face, he lets her. Oh, how he's missed these kinds of touches. He lifts one of his heavy arms responding to her touch. This dark beauty teases him with her laugh and moves just out of his reach. Kick is startled as he hears her trill of glee. After it stops, his only wish for the moment is that she will laugh again. She does, and it's a beautiful sound.

This woman is elegant in her motions and melodic with her amusement. Sensational is the single word Kick pulls out to describe his new obsession. Kick wants to ask her name, but he's too deep into the drug haze to remember in the few seconds it takes to process the words. By that time his body is responding to her hands as she undresses him. He helps her as much as he can and then grabs her hand as she touches his chest. He is sure she said something, but it's lost.

Trix said, "I will thank my brother for you. I wasn't expecting such a luscious piece of meat as a Ceorfan mage. Do you want to be my pet? I'll call you my pet, how is that mage?"

She notices he is trying to listen, so she calms him by kissing his neck. The beauty pulls herself close, almost on top of him to reach the most sensitive areas. She is happy he is so gorgeous. The sexy girl has always been attracted to dark hair and eyes. He's a bad boy fairy-tale. Gortanik is enjoying her being so close to him, but she is enjoying this too. *This will be easier than I believed, I'll make him admire me and do everything I want. He will enjoy me, and I'll enjoy him.* This is just the way things are, whoever she wants—she gets. She rarely wants them as much as they want her, but that's another matter. *This man, this Gortanik, he will remember me. I'll make sure of that. I want him, and he will be mine. She turns up the heat.*

Trix marks her pet's chest with her nails, and he groans with pleasure. She rewards him by sucking on his nipple while twisting and pinching the other. Little nibbles. Easy bites... *This one needs to be hooked first.* Trix moves lower kissing his hard ab muscles on her way to her goal. Even though he is thin, the health-giving druid sleep has brought his warrior physic back and Trix is enjoying his sexy definition. Taking his cock in hand, she pumps a few times then continues her downward motion, pinning his rock hardness to his lower belly. She holds it there with her soft hand while her tongue traces a wide path up and down his shaft. His hands hold her head as he hopes for release. Now she takes the whole tip of his cock in her mouth and sucks pumping with her hand, the wetness of her saliva is making slick sounds while she keeps up a rhythm. He is moving with her, lost in the sex and drugs. She knows his hope is selfish right now, so she slows him. "Gortanik, I need something too," she coos into his ear.

She moves off the bed and stands in front of him where she

performs a striptease. As she removes her top, she holds it close to her, covering her chest while her lips pout and she bites her lower lip. Then lowers her top, exposing her perky breasts to him. Trix pushes the top to her belly and toward her underwear. She drops the top on the ground and lowers her panties as she turns backward exposing her ass to him as she bends all the way over from her waist. Now that she's nude, she stands unashamed, facing him. Here she runs her hands over her body, rubbing in oil that Kick never saw her get. It doesn't matter. He loves the display and never looks away. Rubbing her crotch for him, she asks, "Are you sure you want me?"

If he says no she must leave, that's part of the magic. She must ask the question though. She's never received a "No" answer in all her life.

He pauses... then growls, "Yes, yes I do."

So, she crawls over him and straddles him, rubbing against his dick bringing herself to the edge of orgasm. She guides him into her tight pussy and rocks. In seconds she's coming with him. He passes straight out, exhausted, the drugs are doing their job.

She leans in close to his ear and whispers, "You are mine, my pet, you love me and will do anything I want. You want me any way you can get me, and sex is good every time we fuck."

These words seal her spell over him. But Trix notices that he has other spells on him too. They tingle different from her own. She doesn't know what they are. So, she will get dressed and go to visit her brother, Walter. Maybe he can tell her. Trix knowing her brother, doesn't want Walter to hurt her new pet. She likes him very much, and Walter can be so rough sometimes. She'll warn him, *this one is all mine. He'll help you, Walter. But Gortanik belongs to me. I'll tell him.*

She leaves his room while he sleeps. As she enters the hallway, she meets her friends Sass and Lacie who had just had their ways with Peter and Steen.

Trix smiles a knowing grin at her friends and says, "Mine is gorgeous and has a big cock that thrills me. Are yours as good as mine?"

The other two giggle and Lacie says, "Mine is a doll. He even tried to help. He took the spell and wanted more. What about you, Sass?"

"Oh, I have the best of the bunch his name is Peter. He lives up to his name," Sass cackles, "and I set the spell nice and tight. But you know, my Peter has other spells on him. Do they intend to hurt him? I like him and want him."

"I noticed the same thing. Come with me to talk to my brother. We can ask what these spells are and let him know that we don't want them hurt and if they get rid of them, we want them."

The three satyriatrix find Walter in the dining room having breakfast with Bladriell. As the three walk in, Bladriell chokes on his bite of food as he watches them enter. They're exquisite. Sass is an auburn-haired siren, and Lucy is a vibrant redhead unlike dark Trix and her rainbow hair. Her eyes are green and not blue like her friend's. With a knowing grin toward Bladriell, they sit, and Trix asks Walter about the spells.

He tells them they're not to hurt the men but to control them. A tracking spell and a place spell which is activated by his words and a spell to make them believe that Baratium is still around and not imprisoned. He asks if the drugged mages will do as the satyriatrix promised him. They answer, "Yes," in unison. Trix adds, "But it needs at least a week to set. Then we can test the strength of the magic."

"All right, then you have one week," says Walter, "then we'll have them open the bottle for Baratium's release."

The satyriatrix friends are happy with this news, and they get themselves their food. While she is filling her plate, Trix queries, "Have you told the Fae king and queen of your plans? Will they be helping?"

"The king and queen remain their usual selfish selves and still keep to themselves, offering no help nor providing any hindrance. Still, no matter what, we don't want to make them angry. I'll ask for an audience tomorrow. I'm sure that I'll just be informing them of what is happening. I should also tell them that the plan we have to rid the world of the human pestilence is still on the docket."

They all know that chancing violence at the dark court is never a good idea. It is always better to stay away. Still, in this case, Walter would be in deep trouble if he doesn't tell the rulers what's going on. He doesn't have a choice. "So, everyone is clear, the satyriatrixes will continue with their Ceorfan mages, binding them to them. Bladriell will keep them drugged while I visit the Dark Court."

They all agree with the plan for tomorrow and go their separate ways for the night.

18

THINKING IT OUT

WAKING FROM HIS DRUGGED SLEEP KICK IS SMILING. THAT WAS the most real dream he's had in a long time. That's when he notices his clothes are on the floor and he's sure he has ejaculated, palming his dick there's a definite film. He gets up and feels the sting of the scratches on his chest. When he looks in the mirror, he sees four scratches. Okay, so maybe it was real. The dream woman who had given him so much pleasure... Hopefully, I can dream of her again! On second thought, I'd better forget that, it's disrespectful to Drusey. What I need is to check on the others and take a trip sneaking off to the village in South Africa, where we got the diamonds, to check if they need more food.

Kick bathes, and dresses and heads to Peter's chamber first. He is still asleep, so he leaves him to rest and goes to visit Steen. Steen is finishing getting dressed when Kick knocks on his door. A smiling Steen waves him in and asks, "Are you hungry? I think I can find something to cook us in the kitchen."

"I am ravenous, so yes cook for us. What has gotten into you that has you so happy you're willing to cook this morning?" Kick wonders.

"Well, I think our captors are deciding we have needs and sent me a little fun last night."

"Is that what you call it? I guess you're right though because I had company too and I enjoyed her. But until now I thought I was dreaming it all."

That's when Peter enters the room smiling and says, "So we all got lucky, or the evil mage just out of the kindness of his heart is taking care of us?"

"You're right, it should concern us what this means. Until that time, I'll enjoy the time with the lady. It's been too long since I've heard laughter. I like it. In fact, earlier I decided that I'd like to return to the village where we got the diamonds. I want to be sure they still have food and maybe bring them a goat and teach them to milk. But I'd also like to visit my parents. Do you believe you two can spell me an alarm for when Walter or his minion is on the way? I will portal back in seconds," Kick says.

Peter replies, "But if you do that, they could see the portal as it closes. It would be better if we sneak into the lab while they're gone so you can jump with the jump buoy."

"Come on mages. Let's go to the kitchen. I want to cook and eat something this fine morning," says Steen.

When Kick walks into the kitchen with Steen, he can tell that it was used recently. The smell of the food that was prepared earlier makes his stomach rumble with hunger. He can't even remember the last time food sounded good to him. Steen finds all the makings for pancakes and begins cooking. He makes his own syrup as he is cooking the pancakes. Peter is talking a mile a minute from the sugar buzz when Bladriell enters the kitchen.

"Well, this is different. I guess that your guests have you feeling like men again. Walter will be out today, so will I. Make your own meals and clean up after yourselves. Here is something for each of you. Make sure and take at least a spoonful of this today. In fact, you can have as much as you want. Tell me when you need more. There is plenty in the laboratory," Bladriell informs them while he sets a bottle of an opium concoction in front of each of them.

Kick leaves his without touching it, but the others put theirs in one of their many pockets. He doesn't give Bladriell even the respect of looking at him as he speaks. He certainly will not thank him for the drugs he's addicted to. What he wants is to see his family and doesn't wish to see Peter, or Steen hurt if they catch him. Kick can still sneak away if he thinks it's safe. He asks, "Bladriell, I would like to spend some time with my parents and the Ceorfan queen. I plan to use the jump stone in the laboratory while you're gone. I promise you that I will return."

Bladriell blinks a few times planning what to say. "Well, at least you have the fortitude to ask instead of lie and steal away, Gortanik. But it's useless. You know we're in the realm of the Fae. No one without fae blood can come or go from this realm. Anyway, we long ago found your parents graves when Walter needed to use them against you and the Ceorfan queen is also dead. Her head is on her castle wall as a lesson against her well-earned treachery. He stops, remembering he needs them as friends, when he sees the pain and anger rising on all of their faces he adds, "I am sorry. I should have told you when you woke from the druid sleep. If you let me put a spell on you. I can tell you where the graves are, you can visit there and the castle where the queen's head is located. It will be an easy compulsion spell. One that will compel you to return or everyone around you dies the minute you speak to anyone, and the spell will also be on them. This way Walter will not kill us all, and we won't have to suffer."

Kick is sure that he is putting the spell on his friends to keep him under control. He bites his tongue controlling his anger. "It would be a gift. I will be indebted to you for granting this. I have Fae blood and can travel there and back," he replies.

"Of course, and you two also?" Peter and Steen nod to the assistant who they are trusting to help them. "You will find out that the Ceorfan town of Ageum isn't there anymore they destroyed it a few years after you were all taken captive and not much remains since your captivity, but there is nothing now," Bladriell informs them drawing them into his confidence.

"Come let's go the laboratory so I can set spells on you. Go quick and get back. I will go with Walter today, we'll be gone most of tomorrow also. But I don't want him to catch you if we can avoid it. The master will kill us all."

The mages all stand in the lab talking while the creepy mage's assistant busies himself gathering a stone and a book with the spells to place on the prisoners. He knows he might have made Gortanik upset so to make it up he adjusts the spells so that he can speak to people while he is in the area of the castle and grave. Chanting he puts a stone in Peter's hand. The stone pulses and a green muddy colored light covers him head to toe. The lying mage repeats the same spell on Kick and Steen. When he's finished a bell tinkles in the room and Walter walks in pretending that he doesn't know what they are doing. He does well with the subterfuge because he fools Kick.

He orders them to take their opium. Peter and Steen take the drug out of their pockets and take a big gulp. They want it and are thankful that he ordered them to take it instead of looking weak in front of Kick. However, Kick has left his on the table in the kitchen, so he says he needs go get his. Walter waves at him dismissing him and the others. Something is off, Walter is sure of it, he tells Bladriell to get his cloak they are leaving now for the Faery court.

Bladriell sticks a hand in the air and chants a few words, and his cloak appears. "Ready, Walter."

They leave the room planning to portal from the front of the fortress. When they are sure they can't be overheard, they speak freely. The assistant, "I have a lot to tell you."

"I heard most, they are trusting you. Good job, apprentice." Without preamble, Walter lifts his hands and with a sweep through the air, and they are gone.

19

THE ANGUISH OF LOSS

KICK ENTERS THE EMPTY KITCHEN AND RETRIEVES HIS OPIUM with shaking hands. The smell of the lingering breakfast makes him sick to his stomach. Instead of taking the drug he waits. He can wait and test his strength and resolve. Nodding to himself he heads to Walter's lab and to the jump buoy, his chosen tool to his goal of liberation. He will take the others with him some other time, he berates himself for telling the assistant that he can travel the realm freely. He gave away too much information. But it's a moot point as the spells that he allowed the ass to put on him will hold him prisoner. He pauses and holds onto a nearby table putting his head down; he is nauseous. Not having his drugs makes him weak, he really wanted to wait but it's impossible, so he takes some but cuts down on the dose. It will help until he can wean himself off. Now, he's ready to leave and puts a hand to the buoy and sings his spell.

Kick, arrives at the location Bladriell had given him for his parents' graves. It's a large graveyard, quiet and lonely. He performs a spell to find the graves, singing softly. In seconds he's in front of the stones marking where they are buried. These stones must've been beautiful when they were set. Now, however, they're black with age and moss. Pain! This understanding brings Kick face to face with the knowledge of how long they were in the druid sleep. Weeds surround the monument his parents share. Their epitaph reads, 'They gave their all to retrieve their captive son from the enemy.' Kick sinks to his knees leaning on the stone and weeps. He sings a song of farewell and love to his parent's memories. He stands and cleans the area around the graves. With a handful of grass, he wipes the stone. It's too old, and the grime of the ages stays put. Kick undaunted sings a spell to clean it and in seconds it is gleaming like the day they inscribed it. He finds Peter's parents' headstone and cleans it the same. Steen had no relatives that he knows of, so he doesn't look, but he will ask when he tells them what he's found. Drusey has no monument here, and it hurts him that he can't find where they would remember her.

He says out loud, "Mom, Dad, I'll walk over to find the queen now, and return when I can. I love you."

THEY CEORFAN MAGE wanders around the area to find his former home, only to discover it's gone. The only building left of Ageum is in ruins. It is still recognizable as the temple dedicated to Athena. Kick moves up the hill at a quick pace. He's winded before he arrives at the top, that's irritating. Fuck! He should be stronger. Fighting the demands of his body he can't put off the fix he needs, so he stops long enough to sip a scant bit of the concoction the asshole mage made. Tucking it back into his pocket he detects a man and child walking along the hills. He makes his way over to them, and they strike up a conversation. They are on their way to the castle. They talk to him as they walk then part ways as they reach the castle. He marks that their speech is a little different from what he is used to and files that in his brain for future reference. It reminds him of the way the Ceorfan Queen Kendra from the future was speaking when she was so ill. She had inhabited the body of Queen Leta in his time period. That was so long ago...

And as if thinking of her was enough for the mage to be in her presence, Kick stops dead in his tracks when he sees Leta's great dragon head crusted over and dulled with the same time degradation as his mother's and father's tombstone. His heart aches. A tear runs down his face. He wants to spell the great head clean the way he did the grave marker, but it would be very noticeable. Why would his people leave her displayed in this way? Where are his people? He walks into the city that is around the castle, and none of them are Ceorfan. He asks one of the silk traders, "Do you know where to find the Ceorfan?"

"The what? What is a Ceorfan? There are fans in the market square."

"Okay, where are the gargoyles?"

This time, the man knows what Kick is asking him. He is afraid when he says, "They have one demon on the castle."

Kick speaks with several of the inhabitants. He picks up the differences in the language and even makes a friend of one merchant who offers him coffee. They sit and talk about the man's family for a while until there is no way he can stay longer and says his goodbyes.

He's got one last thing to do though, or rather one last place to visit. It takes him a few minutes to get there but when he does, he easily finds the cave opening he is searching out. It is obvious it's not been used or seen much traffic in all these years. The cave where he and Drusey last met hasn't changed. Kick won't forget the last picnic they had there. His memory supplies all the pictures of the last time they had lain together. It was the night before Baratium murdered her.

He says into the air, "Drusey I miss you. I'll always love you. I'm privileged that you loved me. Right now, I need help to do what is right, and it has been a long time since I have done anything right. I'm hooked on drugs, and my life is reduced to that of a slave. Help me!" He cries into the darkness. The dark headed man drops to his knees, tears streaming from his eyes. The pain of losing Drusey as fresh as if it had happened yesterday. Kick leans forward, hands on his knees, rocking. He lowers his head with his eyes closed and asks one more time, "Please help me." When he opens his eyes, he sees a glint. Nothing special, but it's a glint with a memo. This message says, "Take me." That's exactly what he does, he picks up the item that had reflected the light of the sun into his eyes. He realizes it is an artifact. He looks it over and cleans it up. As he cleans, a sense of elation overtakes him. This time, however, it has nothing to do with the drugs they have plied him with. The little artifact is a hair clip that he'd seen Drusey wear many times. One he had taken from her hair.

"Thank you for the gift. It'll encourage me to be strong enough to do what I need to do, my love. I think I'll be able to live my life now. It would be better to have you, but I can move forward and quit wallowing in my grief. The world has changed so much. I need to find our people and help them any way I can. After I kill Baratium and secure vengeance. Then I'll be free, and I can free Peter and Steen." He puts the hair clip in his own black curls.

Wistfully, he says his last goodbye and sings a phrase jumping back to the buoy in the workshop. Now his body is demanding more of the drugs. He's accustomed to taking more than he has and the last few hours have been difficult. Kick takes a big dose not worrying about his decision to quit taking the drug. He makes it up to the rooms but checks on Peter and Steen before he goes to his own. They are either asleep in their beds or drugged Kick can't tell the difference. As he opens his own door, he half hopes to see the girl from the dream. She isn't there, and he sighs resigning himself to his usual solitary life. He lies on his bed and plans his revenge and freedom from this captivity. He doesn't get very far before he drifts off to sleep.

The drugs still very much in his system he hardly notices as someone cuddles up beside him. He reaches for the person opening his eyes to make sure it's the woman he is dreaming about again. Oh yes, it is his dream sex goddess. She's wearing a red scarf like covering that is hiding nothing. If the intended effect of the covering is to make his blood boil, it is supremely effective.

"Who are you, dream lady?" he inquires.

Trix answers, "I'm just what you need to feel better."

"Please don't tease me. I'll tell you who I am. I'm Gortanik. I might even share what my friends call me if you share your name with me."

"My name is Trix, and I like your name long like your shaft," Trix teases as she plays with his erect penis.

He groans as she gets down to business and leans in to kiss him. His arms draw her close. She isn't soft with the kisses, and her hands are not either as she pinches and twists.

He gets the hint and asks, "So you like it rough, Trix?"

"The rougher, the better," then she begs, "please, be rough," she digs into his chest with her nails.

Not hesitating, he flips her onto her stomach, lifts her up on all fours, tells her to put her hands on the wall, and don't move. He can't see her arch a brow and grin, it's just getting interesting for her. Now he reaches around her and pinches a nipple as he rubs his shaft into her contacting the most sensitive part of her body. When she is panting, she moves a hand, and he slaps her ass with a stinging hit, and he reminds her not to move. She puts the hand back with a smile and moans. Her hair is in his way as he bends to bite her back, so he grabs it and jerks back to hold her head from hitting the headboard as he pounds into her. Stretching her wetness with his cock until they both explode in orgasm. He rolls over, and she still has her hands against the wall panting.

Kick notices and waits for a minute enjoying the view then tells her she can lie next to him as he sleeps. That's what she does, and when he is asleep, she whispers into his ear. "You will get a lot rougher with me so that your un-drugged self will want to owe me. You'll give me everything I want, and I want a lot. You're not just addicted to the opium you are addicted to me. I want more, and want it now, wake and give it to me."

He moans in his sleep and does her bidding like a good boy then rolls back to sleep. "You do that so well my pet. I want you to open the bottle in the laboratory as soon as Bladriell says he wants it opened," she whispers and then leaves to her own room. If she isn't here when he wakes... he'll miss her.

20

PLANS WITHIN PLANS

Walter and Bladriell reach the Dark Court in minutes, but they're held in the foyer by the steward while the guards verify their identities. Which should only take seconds, but this is the fae, and they do everything to show who is in charge. So, they wait. At least, this waiting room is comfortable. There's nothing to eat or drink, it's just lovely furniture to sit on while they wait.

After what seems like hours the steward returns and says they'll set appointments for the royal family in the morning. Walter holds his breath. It would be like this arrogant ass to keep us waiting all day just to tell us to come back tomorrow. It seems the steward is watching Walter, testing, waiting for a reaction. Instead of showing his frustration, Walter does as he should and stands to leave. Satisfied that neither of the two will lose their temper, the guard tells the malevolent mages, "The queen has invited you to dinner with the royal family and you may stay in one of the guest rooms after the meal."

THE DINING HALL is as extravagant as all the palace rooms. Gold and glitter are the main themes. The horrid mages come to understand that this is a strange dinner, even for Walter. It's more a spectacle than entertainment. They prepare the food in front of the guests. Which means they kill the animals in front of them too. At the sight of the slaughter, many of the fae are squealing with pleasure at the sight of the blood and guts from their soon to be dinner. After the animals are cleaned and skinned, the cooks magically clean the remnants of the gore. Afterward, they spell the preparation of the food. Aroma fills the chamber as the meat is prepared with potatoes, loaves of bread, and various mouthwatering vegetables. The food is far better than any food the two have at the fortress garrison by a long shot.

The royal couple is seated far away at a different table in the room's front. Walter can't speak to them even if he tries. When it's obvious, it's over, and the waiters finish clearing the meal a steward introduces himself to them. "My name is Tornitch. I am the royal steward. Please follow me." Walter and Bladriell stand and follow Tornitch. "This is the beverage room. What would you like to drink?"

Walter and Bladriell both know the king is renowned for his brandy. Without hesitation, they both ask for the delight. After consuming several glasses of the caramel and flower flavored drink, Walter searches for the king. However, while the king and queen are in the room, they stay far from Walter. There truly is nothing like fae brandy. Neither mage has ever had anything as good as this brandy. Soon they are quite drunk and retire to their rooms rather than risk embarrassing themselves.

The next morning with a throbbing head Walter wakes Bladriell. Soon afterward, they're told that the king will see them after breakfast. The breakfast is a little more civilized than last night's dinner, but it is no less delicious. Again, after their meal, Tornitch arrives. This time he takes them to the throne room, instead of the beverage lounge. On the way there, the steward shares, "The king and queen are in very good moods. If you don't upset them, you might get your petition answered positively."

Walter and Bladriell don't look at each other. Both know what they have riding on this meeting. They've already discussed their plan for speaking with the king. They merely need to implement it now.

Upon entering the throne room, Walter feels he may have walked into a dream. Damn, if I didn't know I was awake, this room would convince me I was in a dream. Everything in the place seems to have an ethereal quality. Even the air is distinct as it vibrates with magic. Music is everywhere, yet not concentrated in any location. Unless Walter focuses on it, he can't be sure there is any music. Yet, it is present, and the sound moves past them like a gentle breeze, barely noticeable but nice. Fae of every size and breed are in the room flowing in and out of sight, or, is it existence? The royal couple is seated, and Tornitch motions to them and they move forward.

Forgetting the flowing beauty of the court around him isn't easy. The grizzled ass would bet that's part of its purpose too. Walter bows to the king and queen of the Fae. They nod but don't speak. The king turns a hand over showing to Walter he has permission to air his petition.

Walter begins, trying to keep his timbre in quiet even tones and his rhythm unrushed. Still, his voice is grave and rough compared to the gentle sounds of the room. "Your Majesty, I have not come to beg a favor but to inform you of our intentions so that you know all that we are planning and the events about to unfold in the Fae lands belonging to you. I will continue if this pleases you and your beautiful queen." He blinks satisfied with himself sure he's the epitome of decorum.

The king nods to him but with a look that says get it over with and be gone.

Walter continues, "Our master, Baratium Mezacain, was wrongly imprisoned in a spell bottle long ago by the scum of the Earth realm, the

Ceorfan. One of your own people." He points out the injustice of one of their own being imprisoned, as if they didn't know, to impress the issue they already understand. His foot taps to compound his words. He continues, "We have recently gained possession of the bottle. We intend to break the spell and set him free. When we do that he will want to crush the inhabitants of the Earth realm. When he does, I am sure he will share with you the riches of the land that he will rule."

The beautiful fae king smiles a tiny but terrifying smile. With that, he waves a hand dismissively and turns to his wife without looking at Walter again. Walter backs away, and Tornitch is there to show them the way to the door. The steward tells Walter as he hands him his walking stick that he hopes he has a safe trip home and closes the doors of the palace on them before they can say a word in response.

They stand alone in the palace's front. After turning blank looks on each other, the mages leave for home knowing better than to speak now.

THE KING LOOKS at his queen and retorts, "I can't imagine how such an ignoramus can tie his shoelaces, much less release Mezacain."

"Such a hideous creature too, dear. I think none of them will be welcome in my presence again. Do you think we should allow them to destroy the humans?"

"We cut ourselves off from the humans because of the abuses they forced upon our people. We have no reason to change that stance. Besides, why would we need to spend our time worrying about those idiots?" he finishes.

AFTER WALTER and Bladriell reach a safe distance from the palace Walter inquires, "Well, Bladriell, what do you make of that?"

"Walter, when the Fae King smiled I almost shit my pants. That's not someone I want to piss off. I think it's good we came to tell him the plan, but I never want to go back there again. We've got to be sure that when our master takes possession of the Earth, he's good to your word and shares something with the king and queen here. You know how they are about deals. He probably had the words you said to him written somewhere in blood."

"I know how you feel, and you are right we must be sure that master gives something of value to the fae." The two evil mages turn and proceed down the path then take out a small jump buoy and are back at the fortress in a flash.

21

SOLIDIFYING THE LIE

ONCE BACK IN WALTER'S WORKSHOP BLADRIELL LEAVES TO observe what his prisoners are up too. He sits at his desk and uncovers a brass mirror and chants a spell. His creepy ass can then view what he chooses and he resolves to follow the movements of Gortanik first.

He watches Gortanik as he had entered the lab and used the jump buoy to travel to Ageum. The image shows him traveling to his parents' tomb and cleaning their grave markers. The assistant mage writes a note to himself.

1. Force the dark-headed mage to recognize that Baratium is responsible for the deaths of his parents.

2. Note that the master captured the mage in the bottle during that time. This mage was also trying to defend the Ceorfan warrior's parents, and that is the reason Baratium imprisoned him in the bottle.

3. The more that Gortanik believes the lie, the more he'll want to help get the mage out of the bottle as soon as possible.

At this point, Bladriell is especially happy with himself. He decides that adding more information to the plot will increase his odds at receiving help from the three mages. He pens the following to the end of the note;

4. Finally, add that Baratium is afraid of the mage trapped in the bottle because he is very powerful.

BLADRIELL WATCHES the rest of the doings of the Ceorfan mages with reticent imperiousness. He watches as Gortanik sees the orange queen and he hears as the bereft warrior mage calls Drusey's name. But this, to the bored mini-mage, is of little use in controlling Gortanik.

When Bladriell's sure there's nothing else of use, he retrieves the large bottle of the opium that he's used to fill the captive's bottles and takes off to visit each of them. He portals to Peter first and finds him passed out in his room with his beautiful love slave asleep by his side. Peter's small bottle of opium sits empty on the table near his bed. The apprentice fills the empty bottle before moving on to the next prisoner, Steen. He finds Steen in much the same condition. Steen must have a higher tolerance to the drug as he comes around when Bladriell stoppers his little flask of refilled opium.

"There there, my friend, here take a drink of this." And the assistant helps Steen to drink a large draught out of his bottle. Steen slams back into his bed boneless and happy for the drug as his very own satyriatrix enters the room. Bladriell scoots out not wanting to witness what she has planned with her willing victim.

In the hallway he portals to the last of the captives where he finds a different scenario. Gortanik is wide awake and sitting at his desk studying a book that he must have gotten from the fortress' library. He looks up at Bladriell as he enters his room. In shock, Bladriell almost backs out of the room, just stopping himself. He remembers he is faking friendship, so he bows slightly and apologizes for entering without knocking. Trix is nowhere to be seen he discerns and wonders if she is doing her job or not. "I'm sorry for my rude intrusion. It's been a long time since I've found you awake and busy. In fact, this is the first time," stammers Bladriell.

"That's all right apprentice. Did you visit the king and queen? Did you gain information from Walter that'll help us defeat Baratium?" Kick asks coming straight to the point.

Taken aback by Gortanik's brashness, the evil assistant sputters that they did talk with the Fae royalty. He gets his feet under him and he calms then says, "I'm working on Walter. I did find out something of interest. He has a prison bottle hidden in the laboratory that has a mage trapped inside. I'm not sure who it is, but I do know that he's powerful and was defending your parents when the master killed them."

Kick keeps the look on his face blank, but his heart soars. *If I can get the bottle, I know I can release the mage inside. This is what I've been waiting for. I can use this to free us. Afterward, we can make it to the Ceorfan Guild and help them to defeat the fucking douche-bag Baratium and his shit-eating psycho minions.*

Bladriell smiles, feeling the victory he and Walter have searched for nearing. *I'm going to try to get this taken care of now.* Instead of being excited, the creepy mage remains calm and says, "I understand a spell like this take a lot of magic. Maybe I can fool Walter into thinking it's someone we can use to steal more treasure and he'll help us," Bladriell says testing.

Gortanik takes the bait. "I feel that we need to get this done. The more we have, the better chance we'll have for success. See if you can trick him and I'll get Peter and Steen in on the plan. When do you think we should start because I'd like to get this finished as soon as possible?" Kick poses.

"Tonight, if Walter agrees. You're right, the sooner, the better. I'll come back when I've got an answer from Walter. I'll send you a copy of the spells I think we should try when I get to the laboratory and have an answer from our jailer. Let me refill your opium so you can rest today."

Kick hands his bottle to Bladriell who's glad to see that it's as empty as the other mage's bottles were. He had been afraid that Gortanik was trying to stop using the drug. But that'll take a healing only dragons can give. Ha, good thing there are no more dragons. Then he portals back to the laboratory where he and Walter have a great laugh that their plan is falling into place so easily.

22

LETTING THE MAGE FREE

KICK TRIES HARD BUT ISN'T ABLE TO STAY AWAY FROM THE opium. He limits his doses but still spends the afternoon in a haze before he gets around to talking to Peter and Steen. After he convinces them to meet him in his room, he tells them what the creepy apprentice had shared. They agree that they should open the bottle and let the imprisoned mage out. They are sure it's the right thing to do and believe this imprisoned mage must be on their side if the fuckboat Baratium had locked him up. "This is our new mission. We must free this trapped mage at all costs if we want a chance at freedom," Kick says.

Peter and Steen both nod their agreement.

Each of the three does their best to limit doses of opium to prepare for operation 'free our savior.' Yet, they are all so addicted that they're still drugged when Bladriell comes to Kick's room. Yet, they aren't quite in the deep drug stupor that they were yesterday.

Mini-mage Bladriell shares, "Walter doesn't have a clue what he's agreed to do. But he's gonna help us open the bottle tonight. Also, this is the spell we should use. Practice it and commit it to memory." One thing he knows about the warrior mages is that they're brilliant. He knows that drugged or not they'll be able to perform when they speak or sing a spell. "I think we should all have dinner together in the dining room. Then we can go take care of the spell. Think of it, we could be free by this time tomorrow." Bladriell pauses and looks at the others. They don't acknowledge him. "Let's meet around nine or do any of you have a better idea?" Bladriell inquires.

Peter answers, "I think we have committed this spell to memory while you've been blathering on, mage. But you're right we will need all of our energy to perform such a powerful spell. Are you sure that Walter is fooled and will help?"

Bladriell answers him with an evil grin, "I know Walter well. He thinks that he'll be getting an ally who'll steal so much treasure for us that our drugs will not even dent our pocketbooks." He is careful to include himself in this, still trying to convince the three mages that they're on the same side. "I couldn't care less if they like me or not. I've just got to keep them guessing for a few more hours. Then it'll be too late for them!"

Now that they've decided on their course of action, they each go to their rooms to nap and have a little fun with their sexy satyria-trixes. In fact, they can't get to the women fast enough. Kick senses the pull of his body to the lovely Trix. He knows she's standing outside his door waiting for an invitation. He can smell her. The monster inside who's addicted to her body drives him, and he spends the next few hours buried inside her. His body is sated even if he looks like he's been in a fight and lost. He takes a sip of his drugs and sleeps for a while.

Trix rubs his arm and Kick jerks awake. His first thought is that he must get the mage out of the bottle. The drugs are still heavy in his system when he and the others meet in the dining room. The three of them are almost giddy with excitement, ready to put an end to their torment. Soon we'll be free of that shithead Walter, and free of his prison garrison too! Kick and the others eat and enjoy a party atmosphere; the food is drugged, and that's okay. It takes a lot to put them out now, and they're only buzzed and want to get to the lab.

The drugs are the only thing that keeps them from noticing the inconsistencies in the behavior of their captors.

Bladriell and the ladies accompany them to Walter's laboratory. The prison bottle is sitting on the table in the room's middle. What a beauty. That looks like it could have come from Ageum. The green glass with gold trim looks familiar to Kick. It, other than reminding him of his home, reminds him of the love he lost.

Walter begins the ceremony with his usual imperiousness and orders his slaves to do this act for his benefit. Kick, Peter, and Steen all catch each other's eyes, only the briefest of glimpses. At that moment, it unites the three. They are no longer the captives. They are the master. When they get this mighty-mage from the bottle he's frozen inside of, they'll have the final power they need to destroy shit-head Walter and fuckwad Baratium. Kick struggles to cover the pure joy he feels at this moment. He can't let on how happy he is to do this job.

Walter demands, "Do you know the spell?"

"Yes," all of them answer as the ladies stand silently behind them, watching.

"Then let us begin and see this mage," he says and starts to chant in an unintelligible language.

The room darkens, and the candles flicker, but stay lit as he rumbles out the words. The drugs are coursing through the Ceorfan mages, and their eyes see magic swirl in the air. Walter and Bladriell blend their voices. It is electric, like a storm on Kick's skin and he knows it is time for him to add his voice to the spell he sings his part and the bottle hisses and morphs, moving like lava as Peter adds his lilting tones to the magic. Power is growing in the room, and the spell is on point and working. Steen is ready and chants with the others. They can distinguish a voice around the place that isn't one of the team of mages, and they get excited realizing it's the mage they're releasing, the one who will help them kill Baratium.

Something feels off to Kick. He keeps trying to concentrate but is lost in his high of magic and drugs. They're all waving their hands with the spell... the magic is at its apex. The women are dancing around like wild witches. The song is thick and... the bottle becomes a puddle of melted goo, and with a flash of energy it zaps them, throwing them across the room. Where the bottle once stood, stands a man.

The mages hit the walls hard and have been knocked out. All but Kick who for a split second thinks he can see... Baratium.

"No! All this time it was Baratium in the prison, and now we've released him!" Kick's heart sinks, and all hope is gone.

Baratium jumps down off the table and walks over to him. He stands over the prone Kick on the floor and laughs at him as he says, "I knew you would be useful one day worm." Then he waves a hand and Kick's world turns black, and he is left alone, floating on a sea of disappointment and shame.

23

MORE KILLING

Kɪᴄᴋ ɪs ᴜsᴇᴅ ᴛᴏ ᴡᴀᴋɪɴɢ ᴀʟᴏɴᴇ, ʙᴜᴛ ᴛʜɪs ᴛɪᴍᴇ, Tʀɪx ɪs sleeping beside him when he opens his eyes. His head is throbbing. He remembers what he thinks happened last night, but it could have just been a nightmare. He can't be sure... yes, he can, his whole life is a nightmare. Why should last night be any different? Trix is the only satisfaction he has, and even she's a nightmare.

Walter comes to rouse him. "Gortanik, get out of bed. I need you to get ready."

"Get ready for what, Walter?"

"We will jump to a town and steal their wealth," Walter replies nonchalantly. "Also, wake your two friends. Get yourselves presentable and meet me in the Great Hall in one hour." Walter turns and leaves before Kick makes any kind of retort.

The truth is Kick considers making a smart-ass comment but, he doesn't want to dig information from Walter or Bladriell until Peter and Steen are with him. When the three of them are together, Kick reckons, that will be the best time to see if they can get answers.

Kick does as he's told and wakes the other two. They accompany their satyriatrixes them each to their bed. The men each look as bad as he feels. The three speak to each other in quiet tones. "Did you see Baratium return last night?" Kick asks the other two. Neither remembers anything. The blast knocked them out cold. The shock of the fact that the trapped mage is Baratium shakes the other two.

"What have we done?" Being the most common phrase, they repeat as they leave for the Great Hall.

When they arrive, they find Walter and Bladriell already there. Both turn to watch the trio as they enter the room. Kick asks, "Okay, what in the seven's name happened last night?"

Walter laughs.

Bladriell replies through a very sarcastic smile, "You don't remember? Well, you helped us rescue the powerful mage. Now, he'll help us steal the gold, just as I promised."

On cue, Baratium jumps into the room.

Okay, it wasn't a nightmare, this is and it's the bloody end of his life. Kick surmises.

"I owe the three of you a debt of gratitude for assisting my mages, Walter and Bladriell. I'll not destroy someone you love for the lack of respect you showed while I was... absent. However, today I will take you and some of my Crafted to a town. You will steal the entire treasure from this town, leaving nothing behind."

The shock of seeing Baratium standing in front of them is overwhelming for Kick. He watches Peter and Steen and knows they agree. How could we have been so stupid? We failed our family and friends. We failed the world. Kick doesn't even bother to look at Baratium when he asks, "Baratium, you have taken everything from us. It destroys us. We don't need to help you do anything."

Baratium looks at him, utter contempt in his eyes. Then he shifts to masquerading a visage of pity, "Tsk, tsk, Gortanik. You will assist me in everything I request. The effect of not helping will be that I destroy every man, woman, child and every other living being in that town."

Baratium watches as his three captives sink into an even lower level of self-loathing. Kick has decided he is of no further value and believes it'd be best to just die. But the death of a whole town, he can't have that on his conscious. I've done enough evil. However, by doing this evil, I can still protect the people of this town.

Walter has placed the jump buoy from the laboratory here, so Kick is sure they are about to use it. Walter gives them each some large canvas bags the likes of which they've never seen before. After he shows them how to use the compartments, he explains to them where they'll find the treasure they're seeking. "There is a great deal of it that looks like paper, like this." He hands them examples of the local currency. "It's quite valuable. Take all that you find."

The three are prepared and Walter informs, "Master, we are ready."

Baratium waves his hand and chants a short phrase. An army of Crafted march into the room where they are standing.

"Wait, you said a few of them would come. This is an army. Why do we need so many?"

"They are coming because I am testing them, now shut up, we are leaving... now!" shouts Baratium.

When they get to the village Kick doesn't recognize very much and asks Peter and Steen if they recognize some of the items. They know less than he does. He sees a table with a vase of roses on it. On impulse, he takes one and puts it in his pocket. Kick laughs to himself. I can still recognize beauty. Maybe that is what I should focus on for myself. At least I can control a small part of how I feel. Hold on a second. I can do better than that. There is pain in this world. I can't fix it all. But I will control how I choose to let people see me.

Kick can hear and understand the people who're begging for their lives. The Ceorfan mages do their best to follow instructions so that their evil captors will let the townsfolk live. They bag all the money from a large building they have learned is called a bank. It has a large metal room in it that they had to use magic to open. It's a treasure trove of the paper the fuckwit desires. With all that they've found, they are sure Baratium will happily leave the people of the town alive now that he has their treasure.

Once again, they underestimate Baratium, he is... evil. He's now more crazed with hatred for the humans than he was in the past. He waves the Crafted into action. Kick, Peter, and Steen watch as the Crafted kill every man, woman, and child in the town. Drugs can't even make the horror go away.

How are they ever going to help humanity with this madman on the loose? Kick watches as the sick horror unfolds in front of him. Baratium stands in front of him directing the death like a musical conductor. Off to his right, Kick finds a newborn baby. Knowing he has less than a second to act, Kick sends it through the jump buoy to the town in Texas where he'd bought groceries for the South African child. Kick searches for more children to shelter. He only finds a few more before the Crafted complete their gruesome march through the town.

Peter is crying. Steen is like a zombie. Neither can respond to his dutiful attentiveness. "My friends, we can survive. We will find a way out of this horror."

OVER THE NEXT months they aren't able to get out of it though. They can only save a few children every time Baratium goes on a rampage. It's sure now that their captors are trying to exterminate humanity. Even in his drug-induced haze Kick knows this.

The Ceorfan mages take more and more of the opium to escape reality. They still see their dream girls but aren't even sure they're real anymore. In the back of Kick's mind, he's still planning to kill Baratium, Walter, and Bladriell. One day, a way will present itself. He'll find it, and these three will pay. For now, he'll do his best to continue to save children from the blood and gore of the killing fields the best he can. Even one is better than none. He, Peter, and Steen haven't been found out doing this yet, Kick hopes that the grocery store workers are finding families for the children who will care for them.

Kick is wandering the halls when he overhears Walter telling Bladriell, "We've got another village to annihilate tonight. Get the mages ready. We must also make our movements more difficult to predict."

"Why?" Bladriell asks.

"There's a group of humans and Ceorfan who are figuring out how to fight back. Our numbers are too small. We can't win a pitched battle. Go, prepare yourself, then the mages."

Kick goes to Peter and Steen, so they can make their own plans. "Ok, we know what they are doing. We also know if we don't steal for them, they will kill us. Maybe not a terrible thing to do; but if we die, we can't save any lives. So, we will steal. But, every person we come to, we'll jump to Texas." Peter and Steen eagerly agree.

Their plan is working out as best as it can... they have found no one to help yet. The bank is empty except for a guard who they jump. Then they grab all the money from the safe. They are almost ready when Bladriell rushes in and hurries them. "The Ceorfan are here, and if we don't leave now, we will all die. That means you three too because the Ceorfan won't know that you three are captives."

As they rush back out of the bank, Kick finds a group of children. He jumps them to Texas as they rush out of the bank, not caring if Bladriell sees or not.

Kick sees the Crafted demolishing the town and killing everyone they encounter. He sees a group of strangers appear at almost the same second Baratium jumps all of them back to the fortress. Yet, it forces him to leave many of his Crafted behind. He roars his displeasure at Walter. "How did you let them find us?"

Secretly Kick celebrates the loss of the crafted and the idea that someone is fighting Baratium and foiling his plans.

24

PETER IS GONE

THE TORMENTED KICK SITS ALONE IN HIS ROOM contemplating his situation. It's been several days since losing several of the Crafted army to the Ceorfan warriors fighting Baratium. That almost brings a smile to the dark-haired mage's visage. Since that night he's hasn't seen Peter and is worried something is wrong. He doesn't know where Peter is, so he goes to Walter and demands to know what information he has concerning his friend.

When he enters the lab he asks, "Walter, I need to know what you've done with Peter? Where is he?"

Walter answers, "The master has loaned him out to kill some carved bastard who's testing to become a warrior for the Ceorfan. The joke will be famous when Peter takes down the idiot. One of their very own has betrayed them from inside the ranks of their race. As soon as we're able to get their location, we'll destroy the pitiful remnant of the Ceorfan Guild."

"So, you've tricked him is what you're telling me? Peter wouldn't kill one of our own on purpose!" Kick shouts.

Walter laughs at him and returns to his work.

I need to get out of here and help save my people. At the least, I need to let them know about Baratium and his plans. The trick will be getting the tracking/compulsion spells dissolved so he can't hurt any of the Ceorfan.

Bladriell continues where Walter leaves off, "We've found several gargoyles who will do everything we ask—all for power. They want to rule and informed us there is a new queen who's just a pretender. They want her dead. So, the master, complied. What do you think, are we to impede their political squabbles? It serves the master's purpose to help them. The first to go is the one testing. Someone has told us he's the pretender's consort. This will get us even closer to their location. They are hidden. Once we find them, we can kill the last of your kind with the Crafted."

"You can't do that to him!" Kick yells. He charges the mages intending to take them apart.

Walter with a deft move of one hand commands two Crafted to pummel the mage. They do the job well with relish. You would imagine they had a mind of their own... but no it's Walter's will behind the beating.

Walter and Bladriell laugh during the abuse. After waiting for an appropriate interval to pass so that Kick receives a proper beating Walter stops the Crafted. They leave the warrior-mage a bloody pulp on the floor. The shitwad old wizard nudges Kick's face with his foot. "Get up Gortanik. Get out of my laboratory. You're in the way."

Kick drags himself to his knees, and using Walter's table, pulls himself up. Just as he's almost up... Walter pushes him. The Ceorfan warrior collapses back to the floor setting off a new round of laughter from the shithead and his mini-mage. This time, Kick crawls to the door, and out of the two evil mages' way before pulling himself back up and returning to his room without another word.

A plan has presented itself. Kick is trying to piece it together. *If I can figure it out... finding Peter is key and dealing with this opium addiction and the sex addiction, the beatings... and oh wait, all while being forced into constant thieving by psychotic maniacs!* "Shit, shit, shit, motherfucker ass-eater!" He tries to yell but isn't successful. He scans the room, hoping something will help him. "Well, that would have been too convenient," he mumbles to himself as he exhales a deep breath.

After his outburst, he draws himself a bath which he heats with his magic. As he's relaxing in the water, he plunges into his thoughts while cleaning the cuts from his beating. After getting most of the blood off of his body, and before he washes his head and face, he removes Drusey's hair clip from his hair. While he holds it, he remembers her.

Without purposing to do it, he takes the bottle of opium from the shelf and swallows a generous swig. Realizing what he has done, he shakes his head and begins the repetitive mental beat down for failing... again. When he's berated himself, he again glances at the clip. He remembers a specific moment... something his girl said... as if she were standing with him he hears her. The memory her says, "I don't like quitting. I never give up. That's why I want to be a warrior mage. In fact, that's why I love you. You remind me never to give up, Kick. When the training gets too difficult, I watch how you fight through. I know you'll never give up, so neither can I."

He moans, *"I promise you Drusey I won't quit. I'll keep fighting until the three of us are free, and the maniacs who started this are fish food."*

Still wishing Drusey were here to help him plan, he lifts the front of his hair, the part that's always in his eyes along with the sides of his head and clips it back. Kick is getting out of his bath when he spots the silhouette of the beautiful Trix coming into his room. Frustrated, Kick responds, his need obvious to Trix.

She laughs... and says, "That's not for me, Gortanik, I am not Trix." Emerging from pitch black into the light, Sass steps into the room and shuts the door. "I'm sorry to have walked in on you like this. She rakes his body and says, "Well not all sorry. I have to talk to you, and I can't let anyone else know. They have taken my Peter. They promised that after he helped them, I could keep him. I have grown fond of him, and I want him back. Will you help me keep him safe from that vile Baratium and Walter? I know you won't and even shouldn't believe me. But I want to help find him."

Kick stands there in total shock. Of any eventuality he had ever considered, one of the satyriatrix's working against Walter wasn't one. Kick stuttered, "Ahem, okay. I have no plan, but.... why do you want to help me, us... I mean, why do you want to help Peter?"

"He is good to me. Just like you are to Trix. She tells me how nice you are to her. Peter is kind to me too, even more, kind I would bet. I'm not saying he's better. I, uh, I don't know how to say it to you." She looks down, and her red locks shield her face.

"Sass, they have held us captive and tortured us for hundreds of years. They've forced us to do horrible things. Things that made us less than human. I need to know why?"

"Well, I guess it's because my nature has defined me for my entire life. Men like Walter always use me for their desires. Peter doesn't see me as a thing to use and discard. He treats me like a person."

A kindred empathy seems to settle between them. For once, Kick sees how alike their situation is. "I understand Sass, but I know nothing other than Walter said they lent him out to kill a newly carved gargoyle. I don't know where it is."

"Well then, I'll try to find information and bring it to you. You can't tell anyone, not even Steen, where you're getting it from. If Walter finds out I'm helping you, he'll kill me, and there's nothing I can do to stop him."

"I understand. When you learn something helpful, tell me. I can't find you, you must check in every occasion."

"Thank you, Gortanik. I have one more thing." She reaches into a small pouch on her hip and removes a small stone which seems to glow a light blue color. "I don't know for sure what it is, but I know the last Ceorfan dragon queen had it, and they told me to not let any of you see it. Maybe you can use it. Maybe this will remove your doubts that I'm telling you the truth."

Sass turns and leaves his room, checking the corridor before slipping out.

Kick turns the stone over and over in his hand. The small smile growing larger. "I know exactly what this is!" Kick says to the empty room.

The excited Kick goes to Steen's room and asks him, "Will you watch over me, so I'm not discovered while I dream-walk and look for Peter?"

"Do you think you can still do it with... with all the drugs we're using?"

Kick shrugs his shoulders then nods. Steen returns the nod and sits beside Kick as he settles into a hypnotic sleep to dream walk. Steen keeps guard.

In Kick's drug-induced sleep he can see a thread that leads to the other two mages. The short one must be to Steen, so he follows the other much longer one. In his vision Kick flies along long stretches of the thread walking where it isn't possible to fly. Eventually, Kick reaches the end of the string. When he finds it... it disappears. It ends with nothing attached at the end. Usually, he sees a person at the end of a thread. But not this time, no Peter.

Kick elects to wait at the spot on the hill where the thread ends. He sits in his dream state and waits. Not sure what he's waiting on but hoping he will know it when he sees it. Then he does... he sees several gargoyle warriors. His heart speeds up as he recognizes Kino as one. Holy fuck! I thought he was dead. The dream walker could not be happier as he watches. They look like Elites but dressed in tight black clothes. A beautiful woman is with them. He watches as they jump into the sky and fly fast and hard into the night.

Smiling Kick now knows where the hidden Ceorfan are. He'll go tell Steen and together they'll work out a plan to get him into the cave to get help.

He feels magic tingle an alarm and wakes from the excursion. Steen has wakened him, so he sends him a questioning look without speaking. Steen gives a subtle point of his chin. When Kick looks over, he sees Trix just coming into his room.

For cover, he says, "And that my dear friend is how you trap a rabbit in the desert." Which is their code for I'll talk to you later.

He glances at Trix and makes like he is happy to see her... and he doesn't mind the time he spends with her. It's better than hot.

Kick says, "Let me spend time with the lady, my friend."

This has Steen grinning, something he rarely did even before their captivity. It's kinda scary looking. The couple leaves Steen to go find his own satyriatrix.

Kick thinks back to his encounter earlier with Sass, and he invites Trix to come sit on the bed beside him. He says, "Trix, I haven't been doing a great job with my friends here. I mean to correct that, beginning with you. Thank you for being here with me and giving me pleasure. You're the brightest spot in this horrid place. Is there something I can do for you? I have little, but I'll do what I can." He gets up and walks to a table in his room where he had put the rose he'd taken from the village earlier. He's been keeping it beautiful magically. He takes the rose from the table. "I know it isn't much, I saw this and thought of you. It's so beautiful and soft but survives... the wonderful scent is but one gift. He pricks his finger on a thorn and continues, "Yes, the more I think of it, the more it is like you." Kick hands her the rose.

The totality of the shock on Trix's face is surprising to Kick, so he kneels in front of her.

"Trix, did I do it wrong?" he asks as a tear slides down her face.

"No Gortanik. Now, I want a kiss to go with the flower."

He leans into her and brushes her lips with his, and their passion heats to the point of no return. He waves a hand and the door shuts and Trix giggles. That's different too. She's usually with people who're so intent on sex they never notice if they have privacy or not. This means a lot to her. Yes, the little things matter. So much that her ideas of this man are turning to how to help him instead of hurting him. *What Walter wanted me to do is done. He got that awful*

Baratium out of prison. I should do what I want now. Yes, new job...
make Trix happy with her pet.

When he is sure, Trix is gone after their sex filled hours. Kick makes his way to Steen's room. The two stay up talking until the need for more drugs takes them, and they separate again. Kick shared the location of the cave and everything else he saw, including the beautiful dragon lady. Their plan now taking form, hope blooms for them both. Kick stresses, "Steen, tomorrow if I don't return with Peter soon, you need to go to Walter's laboratory and use the jump buoy. Jump to where I showed you the Ceorfan gargoyles are hiding. Get help."

25

CAPTURED BY HIS OWN

Both of the Ceorfan mage's hope has been sparked, put out, and relit the last few days. Steen has spent most of the day in Kick's room working on their plan for freedom. "First, we need to find Peter. That means I need to take another dream walk while you keep an eye out for trouble," Kick says.

"Got it," Steen replies. "What do you think the chances are he's alive?"

"I'm guessing he didn't kill the Carved they had sent him to kill. Or if he did, they also killed him. I don't believe they killed him because I still see the life string leading to him. There isn't anything on the end. The best I can say is I hope he's still alive. If he is alive, I hope he hasn't spoken a word if he's with the Ceorfan Guild gargoyles."

"Agreed, if he speaks, it'll start the tracking spells, leading Walter to his exact location. I'm guessing that battle could hurt or kill many of their people. Are you ready?" Steen finishes.

The dream state comes faster for Kick this time. Not to mention, he knows where he's going. This time Kick follows the thread into the cave where he finds Peter. The room is low in a large cave. It includes several rows of cells with two in the back. Peter's in the larger of the back cells. The prison is protected with no way to bypass the locks and spells holding his friend. Peter can't see him, so no message is possible in his dream walk state. Kick will have to go physically to this cave to rescue Peter. He wakes and tells Steen what he found out.

"I think we should jump you there. I'll wait for you to come back, so Bat-head and his slave duo won't know you're gone until it's too late," Steen suggests. Kick grins at the name calling and comes up with one of his own. "I agree. But go to your chamber and take a large dose of opium. That way Fuck-a-rat-ium, and the two shits won't think you know what's happened."

"Good idea. Good luck my brother," Steen agrees.

"Steen, wait..." Steen turns to face his friend. "Do me a favor, be nice to your satyriatrix, Lacie. Also, be nice to Sass. I assume she'll help us, she's in love with Peter. If I don't return, you have been the best of friends."

Steen raises an eyebrow, nods, and answers with a simple, "Okay." Then he leaves.

After Steen leaves the laboratory, Kick wastes no time. Peter has been gone at least a week, and Kick wants to get to him as fast as he can. Kick's lined up several of the Crafted to take with him. He can still order them to do his bidding because Walter has never taken that spell away from him. He's hoping the Ceorfan gargoyles can investigate them and shut them down fast. When he reaches the buoy in Walter's laboratory, he touches it and jumps himself and the small group of Crafted into the cave where he saw the gargoyles and dragon lady leave.

If these are the Ceorfan who live here, I'm positive they'll want to use the Crafted to reverse their magic and destroy them all at the same time. Then I will help them find Baratium and destroy him Walter and Bladriell.

Kick looks around and finds he is inside the cave but not in an area where anyone lives. The smell here is as bad as some places in the fortress. He lights his hand, so he can see better. The light helps, but the room is so large, the light is quickly lost. This must be the correct area... but it doesn't look right. He's afraid he will have to walk around a while to find Peter because now this really doesn't look like the right place at all. *I genuinely need to practice my jump skills!*

It puzzles him and he turns in a circle, hoping to find his way. He can't. He's lost. Taking a deep breath, he stops. He waves the Crafted to inaction, so he can dream walk to find Peter's thread again and watch where to follow it this time. The Crafted aren't moving. Kick sits and leans against a smooth rock. Soon he's asleep and following the thread to find Peter. In the dream's beginning walk Kick finds a large city. He looks around amazed. He sees many Ceorfan. The gargoyles are easy to spot, and he gets excited to see them. The joy he feels is overflowing yet strange and somewhat empty to him after so long with no hope or happiness... or Drusey. It would be great to live among his people again. Longing beats at him like a hammer.

Motivated he continues his walk to find his friend. As he rounds a corner, he sees a group of warriors who look familiar. Kick does a double take. Yes! He sees a gargoyle who he recognizes as one of his commander trainers, Commander Jacobs. There's also a mage he is familiar with. It's Jericho, his old friend, and mentor! Kick is so happy and excited he forgets his pain. *I'll follow them. Jericho will know what to do to help. I'll tell Commander Jacobs... nothing. It'll bring all hell down on these people if I speak. It'll start the tracking and other spells that are on me. Baratium will jump his Crafted army on top of these people before they can react. Wait, they're coming to the area close by where I'm sleeping. Wake up now!*

Kick's opens his eyes and rises just when he sees Jericho coming at him with a spell ready. Kick waves the Crafted into action so they can defend him. *I've got to let them know I'm here in peace. I'm here to help! I have to protect myself, or Jericho will disable me before I have a chance to tell them about the spells on me. No second thought, I need to be captured. They have kept Peter locked safely away, so the tracking spells weren't activated. Besides, maybe they'll take me to Peter. This is amazing. My nightmare is almost over.*

Kick softens a spell and throws it at Commander Mica spinning to launch a kick to his nether region. *Guys watch me, watch my face. Evaluate me. I'm not here to hurt anyone. I'm here to help and be helped. Wait, please! I have to tell them about Steen. Never mind, they will fight me full-on. I can't fight them, but I have to, at least so I can tell them about Steen.* Jericho takes over the fight with him and sends a spell for which the intruding mage has no defense. Kick has seen nothing like it. He feels himself falling. Before he blacks out, he wonders again, What about Steen? He hasn't the strength he once had, and the battle has taken what little energy he had left. He is seriously out-manned.

26

SITTING IN PRISON AGAIN

KICK WAKES LYING IN A BED IN A STRANGE BUT WONDERFUL prison. He and Peter can speak using a type of Ceorfan Warrior sign language. They keep this to a minimum for safety sake. Right now, he knows that they feed them both well and the protection spells on the cells keep them all alive. They're both worried about getting back to rescue Steen and will be glad if someone would take off the spells Walter and Bladriell have on them. Right now, Kick's just happy that they protect the cells so well that he isn't endangering the people he loves. The food they give him is the best since his mother cooked for him, another time, another life.

These are Kick's people. He'll protect them even from himself and the spells attached to him. But it's so different here, it's different now. Will these Ceorfan accept him? That's Kick's reality now. *They might not want me at all! Will I be forced to Hewn status? They think I attacked them. Will they let me live after I'm able to tell my story... if I'm ever able to. I can only hurt the people here if I speak or at least until they figure out how to un-attach the tracking spells. I'm guessing they've stopped using the Warrior Mage Guard because I have seen no one who knows the sign language except Peter.*

He's been here for days and is panicking that they'll leave him here and he won't be able to get to Steen. Kick looks up as someone enters the prison. He breathes a sigh of relief when he sees it is Kino. Then behind him walks the most beautiful woman he's ever seen. Kick never takes his eyes from her but knows several others are with her. She's watching him, a friendly expression on her face. Once again, he has hope. She's the dragon he saw with Kino the day he found the cave.

Please if you are listening at all, Creator give me favor with this woman. This is what he's been waiting for. Now if he can just keep them all safe. He puts his hands against the barrier wanting to touch her then hangs his head. He remembers he isn't good enough for anyone much less this beauty, this dragon queen standing in front of him. So, he makes a solemn vow to himself. *I'll protect her and do her bidding to the best of my ability. I'll hope against all odds she's willing to let someone help me get my revenge on the wooden enemy army and the evil mages who helped make me into a man who isn't worthy to be loved.* He sighs with relief knowing this is the end of his captivity with Walter and Baratium. But in reality, like all things which end... this is genuinely only the *beginning*!

ACKNOWLEDGMENTS

Thank you, our fans and readers of the Ceorfan Gargoyles Series and Novellas. We appreciate each and every one of you. You are our prize. Please, if you enjoyed the books at all consider leaving us a review. It means more than you can imagine! But if you really hate them... please pass.

My family who is always supportive and helpful. Especially Robert and his wife Peggy. My husband, I love that you are in my corner. Thank you, Mom and Pop, for always being here for me. Thank you, Dad for giving me a great imagination. My son and his wife Kit and LaRay, my son Kyle, my daughter in law Callie, and my stepsons John and Jeffery, you are amazing. All my grandchildren you help me keep going. Our cousins are wonderful for letting us write about them! I hope everyone has people in their lives that are as amazing as you all. We are blessed to have you!

All my friends who are precious to me. Miki and Mine Guys and Goyles! A Special thanks for those of you goyles who provided name suggestions for characters. Walter Carr this means you man – Walter, your namesake, hehe. Also, for Kayla Poe - Bladriell, Dene Ward - Slade, Teresa Ebbs - Mezacain, Brandi Bell - Deveros.

Christina and Brenda, you are the best PA's ever!

Craig and Rob, you make everything in this so much more possible. What good dragons! You have always been my best friends. Garrett you really are the best co-author ever! I love you all. Thank you for your support! — Miki Ward

Thank you fans and supporters. Miki said it perfectly above. I could repeat it here. But who'd want to read it again? I will say, thanks for giving us the opportunity to play around with your feelings for a bit.

To my beautiful wife Kathi, without you I am not a person. To my children, thanks for the pure joy, and terror, you continually provide. Because of you, I push myself to a higher standard and sometimes, near the edge of a cliff... To my adopted children, Ethan and Kasia, thank you for making my family, your family. I love you all beyond measure.

To my much older sister and my really little brother, thanks for not allowing me to follow through with my nefarious plans which I'd concocted in my youth. Still, had you allowed me, we'd all have huge houses and buffalo in our backyards!

To my Sangre de Cristo High School friends, I can't believe it's been this long. I also can't believe how amazing you are. Thank you for the fathomless love and support you've freely given me over the last four decades. — Garrett V. Ward

OTHER BOOKS BY MIKI AND GARRETT WARD

The Ceorfan Gargoyles Series

Carved

Etched

Hewn

The Ceorfan Gargoyle Novellas

My Tormented Mage

Ceorfan Teens

Shivers Series

We See You

Double Mirror

Elser Books are stand alone

Flesh and Bold

Stand alone by Miki Ward

My Phantom Queen

FIND US LINKS

Facebook

Miki & Mine, Guys and Goyles Group

https://bit.ly/2CpH3BM

Miki's FB Author page

https://bit.ly/2yMlVSG

Garrett's FB Author page

https://bit.ly/2P3USwv

Bookbub

https://bit.ly/2J3FRFh

Amazon Author Page - Follow Miki

https://amzn.to/2Ey3qrk

Amazon Author Page - Follow Garrett

https://amzn.to/2yNYOr7

Instagram

https://bit.ly/2Ro5utp